A LOVE THAT HEALS THE HEART

Men of Valor
Book Four

By Laura Landon

ARE YOU SIGNED UP FOR DRAGONBLADE'S BLOG?

You'll get the latest news and information on exclusive giveaways, exclusive excerpts, coming releases, sales, free books, cover reveals and more.

Check out our complete list of authors, too!

No spam, no junk. That's a promise!

Sign Up Here

www.dragonbladepublishing.com

Dearest Reader;

Thank you for your support of a small press. At Dragonblade Publishing, we strive to bring you the highest quality Historical Romance from some of the best authors in the business. Without your support, there is no 'us', so we sincerely hope you adore these stories and find some new favorite authors along the way.

Happy Reading!

CEO, Dragonblade Publishing

Additional Dragonblade books by Author Laura Landon

Men of Valor Series
A Love For All Time (Book 1)
A Love That Knows No Bounds (Book 2)
A Love That's Worth The Risk (Book 3)
A Love That Heals the Heart (Book 4)

PROLOGUE

"**I**'LL RACE YOU to the stream, Charlie," Mariah called out to her brother.

"No, Mariah. We'd have to jump the hedgerow, and you're not experienced enough yet. Father said you must be older before he'll allow you to jump over a hedge that tall."

"I'm as old as you were when you started jumping over this hedgerow. Besides, I've been practicing for a week and more."

The expression on Charlie's face turned dark. "Who allowed you to jump this hedgerow?" he demanded.

"No one," she said hesitantly.

"What did you just say?"

"I said, no one," she admitted in a more defiant voice. "I'm not a baby, Charles. I don't need anyone to hold my hand. Besides, how can I get better if I have to wait around for you to trail along behind me as if I were a toddler on leading strings?"

"You *are* a toddler on leading strings!" he yelled back at her. "At least where horses are concerned. You aren't even sixteen, Mariah. You haven't been riding all that long."

"And whose fault is that? Father treats me as if I were a baby, and all Mama wants me to do is stay indoors and play the pianoforte and practice my embroidery. I want to be out in the fresh air. I want to ride like you do."

Charlie laughed. "You want to ride well enough to follow

Jonah around when he comes over. I know you're sweet on him."

"That's not fair. I want to be able to go out riding whenever I want."

"I can't say I blame you," he said. "I wouldn't like to be cooped up in the house with Bach and Mozart as my only entertainment."

"I knew you'd understand, Charlie. You're the best brother I could ask for. Will you race with me?"

He hesitated long enough that Mariah knew he'd give in if she begged long enough.

"Just to the big tree," he finally agreed. "No farther."

"But we won't reach the hedgerow if we stop at the big tree. I won't be able to show you how well I've learned to jump. I'm getting really good, Charlie."

"I'm sure you are, Mari. But not today. And I don't want you to jump that hedgerow yet. It's too tall. You'll be in big trouble if Father finds out you already have."

Mariah knew better than to argue with her brother. The firmness in his voice told her how serious he was. But she really wanted to show him how much she'd improved.

"Are you ready, Mari?"

"Yes." She tightened her hold on the reins and got ready to start.

"Ready," Charlie said.

"Set."

"Go!"

Bridles jingled and tails swished as the two horses leaped forward at their riders' commands.

Mariah took an early lead. She loved the feel of the wind blowing in her face and whipping her hair. She loved the freedom she felt when she raced. It was like flying. Almost like soaring through the sky.

They galloped across the meadow, avoiding the soft ground that lined the gully. She and Charlie raced neck and neck, each horse's nose nearly even with the other. They seemed perfectly matched. That is, unless Charlie was holding back so he wouldn't beat her by too great a margin.

Mariah laughed, thrilled with the thought of besting her brother. She dug her heels into her horse's sides, and was pleased with the response. They were almost to the tree. Almost to the spot where Charlie intended their race to end. But Mariah had no intention of stopping. The hedgerow was just ahead. She'd force Charlie to jump it with her if he intended to win.

She was desperate to show him how good she was. Desperate to prove to him that she was almost as good as he was. She wasn't perfect yet, but she was close. With a little more practice, she would beat him outright.

"Mari! Slow down!"

Mariah heard his shouts of warning from beside her. But she didn't slow down. If anything, she pushed her horse to go even faster.

She surged ahead of him, then prepared for her jump.

"Mari! No!"

Mariah looked to her right and saw that Charlie was so close to her she could almost reach out and touch him. They were going to jump in tandem. It would be magnificent. She'd never experienced anything so euphoric!

Her horse's hooves left the ground, and she soared with him over the hedgerow. Charlie's horse did the same. Except something unexpected happened. Mariah's horse veered to the left and collided with Charlie's.

Both horses screamed. The sky shifted above them, and the ground came up and slammed into Mariah. The pain was excruciating. Her horse landed on top of her and she couldn't breathe.

Charlie released a painful cry.

Then the hillside was silent.

Mariah tried to move, but the saddle ground into her middle. Her horse had her pinned to the ground.

Gritting her teeth against the pain, she turned her head to

focus on her brother. But all she saw was blood. A great deal of blood. Both hers and his.

"Charlie?" she whispered as loudly as she could, but he lay as still as death beside her and didn't respond.

She called out again. Then again. But he didn't answer. The world around her stilled, and she gave up her struggle. She was suddenly too tired, too weak to speak.

Mariah closed her eyes and let the darkness engulf her.

SOUNDS SHE RECOGNIZED as voices grew louder in her ear. Mariah struggled to understand the words being spoken around her, but she was unable to make sense of them. Her brain was so foggy that she couldn't focus enough to understand what anyone was saying.

She thought one of the voices belonged to her mother, but she wasn't sure. There was something different in her mother's tone. It sounded like she was crying.

Mariah tried to tell her mother not to cry, but she couldn't form the words. Then she heard her father comfort her mother. Mariah was glad. He would know what to say. He always did.

"I'm going to take Dr. Nelson down and get him something to eat, Harriet," her father said. "I'm sure he would appreciate some food and a few moments of rest. He's been on his feet all night."

"Do you want me to come with you, Everett?" her mother asked.

"No. You stay here with the children."

"Oh, Everett. How will we survive if we lose them? I'm not sure I can."

"Don't even think that, Harriet. Charles and Mariah are both strong. They'll survive. I just can't imagine why Charles would have allowed Mariah to take such a chance. He knew I had forbidden her to jump that hedgerow. She's not experienced enough."

"I'm so frightened! Charles is injured so terribly. Even the doctor doubts he'll survive."

"He'll survive, Harriet. He has to. He's the future Earl of Aspen."

Mariah tried to open her eyes. She struggled to speak. She wanted to tell her parents that jumping the hedgerow wasn't Charlie's fault. She wanted them to know that she was the one who'd forced him to jump that hedge. She wanted them to know that if her brother didn't survive, it was her fault. But she couldn't. She couldn't stay awake long enough to say the words.

MARIAH STRUGGLED TO waken. Once her body began to cooperate, she slowly climbed out of bed and made her way to her bedroom door by hanging onto anything that would support her. It was important that she go to Charlie's bedroom and be with him. She feared if she didn't stay by his side, he would give up.

He was in an immense amount of pain, much more severe than her own. Last night when she sat with him, he told her his pain was so bad that he didn't think he could stand it any longer. Mariah was afraid he would give up and stop breathing.

She had to do something to help him, so she poured some of the medicine the doctor had left for him in a glass of wine and held it to his lips while he drank it.

He seemed better after that. Although his words were slurred and he seemed lethargic, at least he was out of the intense pain.

"Thank you, Mari," Charlie gasped. "I don't know…what I'd do…without you."

Mariah sat in a chair beside Charlie's bed when she was too weak to stand any longer. "I'll take care of you, Charlie," she said. "I didn't mean to cause my horse to run into yours."

"It's not your fault, Mari. I knew not to let you...jump that hedgerow."

Mariah reached for his hand and held it. "I should have waited until I was better at jumping. I just wanted—"

Just then, the door opened and their mother entered. "What are you doing out of bed, Mariah?" Her mother's voice was harsh. Scolding. "Didn't you listen to Dr. Nelson? He warned you not to get out of bed."

"I just wanted to check on Charlie, Mama."

"That's the kind of recklessness that will cause you to do yourself harm, Mariah."

It was difficult, forcing herself to listen to her mother's warnings, but suddenly a searing pain shot through her. She clutched at her stomach as the piercing pain took her breath. "Mama!" she cried.

"Mariah! What's wrong?"

"Mama!" she panted, then doubled over in pain.

"Come with me. I'll get you back to bed."

Her mother helped her to her feet, and Mariah managed one step before her legs buckled beneath her. The burning pain was so intense that she couldn't bear it.

"Mariah!" her mother gasped.

Then Mariah lowered her gaze to the wet warmth that was running down her leg. There was more blood than she'd ever seen in her life.

Her mother screamed for help, and two maids ran into the room with her father at their heels. He gazed at the pool of blood on the floor and ordered one of the maids to send for the doctor. Then he lifted Mariah into his arms and carried her to her own bed.

"Papa," Mariah said weakly. Though she tried, she found it impossible to speak any louder.

"You have to be strong, Mariah," her father said as he laid her on the bed.

"Papa, will you stay with me?"

"Of course I will, my darling."

"I don't want to die alone."

"You're not going to die, my princess. I won't allow it. Do you hear me?"

"Yes, Papa," she whispered. "Don't blame Charlie. He told me…not to jump…but I wouldn't…listen."

"Shh. It's all right.

"I love you, Papa."

"I know you do, princess," her father answered in a thick voice. "I love you too."

"Tell Mama…I love her…"

Mariah didn't finish her sentence. She couldn't.

She closed her eyes and lost consciousness.

CHAPTER ONE

J ONAH REYNOLDS WAITED for his carriage to stop in front of his
brother's townhouse before stepping to the ground. He took in
the familiar pillars as well as the shaded portico and felt a stabbing
of longing at coming home. He hadn't returned in nearly ten
years, not since his father had demanded he remove himself from
his sight and never return.

It had been intolerable to his father that a son of nobility
could wish to become something as lowly and undignified as a
doctor. He had never forgiven Jonah for pursuing his dream.

Even though his father, Viscount Darbringth, had been dead
these past six years, Jonah had honored his wishes and never
returned. Not even for his father's burial.

But now his brother Russell, the current Viscount Darbringth, had written asking him to return. He didn't know the
reason for Russell's request, other than it must be of the utmost
importance. Whatever it was would no doubt be revealed to him
when they spoke.

At first, Jonah had considered refusing to return to Darbringth House. After all, Russell hadn't once written to him in all
the years since he'd been disowned by their father. But time
healed most wounds. He had no quarrel with Russell, so how
could he refuse such a request? Russell was his brother, his only
sibling, and there had never been any animosity between them.

They'd been close when they were younger. There was nothing Jonah wanted more than to see his brother again and grow close like they'd once been.

He stood on the pavement in front of the Darbringth townhouse and lifted his gaze to the opening front door. Instead of a butler standing in the open doorway, Russell stood there to meet him.

"Jonah," his brother bellowed.

"Russell," Jonah answered, then closed the gap that separated them in long, eager footsteps. He clasped his arms around his brother, and Russell returned his gesture with a welcoming hug.

"I'm so glad you've arrived," Russell said. "It's been far too long since we've seen each other."

"Yes, it has. Far too long."

"Come in," Russell said, wrapping his arm around Jonah's shoulder and leading him inside. "We have so much to catch up on."

Jonah entered the townhouse at his brother's side and perused his surroundings. Not much had changed since he'd left, except a fresh coat of paint and an updated portrait or two on the walls leading up the staircase.

"Does it look the same?"

"Yes," Jonah said. "The same round table is in the middle of the foyer. Even the flowers on the table are the same color, I think."

Russell grinned. "I'm glad you noticed. I tried to remember what color Father always insisted upon for this spot. I wanted everything to remind you of the home you left."

"You have, Russ. Everything is perfect."

The two brothers shared a smile. "Now, come with me. I have someone I want you to meet."

Russell clasped Jonah on the shoulder and led him to the room they had always called the blue room. It was the most formal of the receiving rooms, reserved for special guests.

"Jonah, may I introduce my wife, Lady Julia Darbringth,

Viscountess Darbringth, and my daughters, Alexandra, Daphne, Eugenia, and the baby, Rosalind."

Jonah noticed the loving expression on his brother's face when he looked at his wife and daughters. It was the same look his friends Quinn, Jack, and Theo wore when they looked at their wives—an expression overflowing with love and respect. He was glad to know that Russell and his wife enjoyed a love match, pleased to see that his brother had found a partner who suited him so perfectly.

"Lady Darbringth." Jonah smiled. "It's a pleasure to meet you."

"Please, call me Julia," she replied. "Russell has spoken of you so often that I feel as if we're longtime friends."

"Then you must call me Jonah. I insist."

Russell's wife smiled, and the whole room brightened. Julia Reynolds was a rare gem, and he was happy for his brother.

"Allie is our eldest," Russell said, standing proudly behind the row of young ladies. "She is seven."

"Miss Alexandra," Jonah said with a formal nod.

"And Eugenia here is five."

"Miss Eugenia," Jonah acknowledged with a regal bow.

"And Daphne. She is three."

"Miss Daphne," Jonah said, then smiled when the little tot struggled to curtsy.

"And finally, Rosie," Russell said. "She will be one next month."

Jonah took the babe's fingers and brought them to his lips. "What a beautiful family you have, Lord and Lady Darbringth."

"Thank you, Jonah," Russell said. "I owe their beauty and intelligence to my wife. She shared all her best qualities with them."

"That's not true, Russell," Julia said. "As your brother can see, more than one of them resemble you in looks."

"I can see they are remarkable children," Jonah replied. "I'm sure you are very pleased with them."

"I am," Russell said, then reached for his wife's hand and brought it to his lips.

"How long do you promise to stay with us, Jonah?" Julia asked. "Through the Season, I hope."

Jonah considered his answer. He'd finished training two new doctors to take over for him while he was absent and felt quite comfortable with them in charge of the hospital. It would do them good to be on their own for at least a month or two without him watching over their shoulders. And he'd instructed them to write if something went awry and they needed him to return.

"That is my intention, Julia," Jonah answered. "Unless, of course, you tire of me before then and suggest I return to my hospital."

"Hospital? You run a hospital?"

"Yes. One I'm very proud of. I'll have to tell you all about it."

"I can't wait to hear every detail. But now," Julia said when baby Rosalind began to fuss. "I think it's time to go upstairs with the girls, Polly," Julia said to the nursemaid.

Russell stepped forward and kissed each child on the cheek. "Sweet dreams, rascals."

"Cover your ears, children," Russell's wife laughed, then nodded for the nurse to take the children to their tea.

When the room was once again quiet, Julia stepped to Jonah and reached for his hands. She clasped them in a heartfelt grasp and graced him with a smile so sincere that he couldn't help but be moved by her graciousness. She was truly a special woman, and his brother was fortunate indeed to have her as his wife.

"I can't tell you how pleased I am that you've come to stay for a while, Jonah. I know Russell has looked forward to it for a very long time. And so have I."

"Thank you, my lady," Jonah answered. "I look forward to my time here. Russell and I have much to catch up on. And you have made me feel ever so welcome."

Russell stepped to her, wrapped his arm around her, and held her close. "Is my Julia not the perfect wife, Jonah?"

"She is indeed," Jonah answered sincerely. "You're a lucky man, brother."

He felt a stabbing of regret when he realized he'd never experienced such a feeling, and doubted he ever would. He was past thirty and had never met a female who stirred even the slightest interest in him. At his age, he doubted he ever would.

"I believe I will check on the girls now and leave you two to catch up with one another," Julia said.

Russell walked with his wife to the door, and when he returned, he stopped at the sideboard and poured two glasses of brandy. He handed one to Jonah, then sat down opposite him.

"You are extremely fortunate, Russell," Jonah said. "You have a beautiful family. Your wife is remarkable and your children are precious."

Russell took a swallow of brandy. "Yes, I am exceedingly blessed. Julia is the love of my life. I don't know how I would survive if something happened to her. I was so fortunate to have found her."

Jonah studied the frown on his brother's face. "So why is it that I sense something is wrong, Russell?"

"Nothing is wrong but—" Russell started to say, then paused. He lifted his gaze and locked it with Jonah's. "Yes, Jonah. Something is wrong."

"What is it?"

"I wasn't going to bring this up just yet. I was going to wait until you had been here at least a few days, but I find I can't. I need to confide something to you, as it involves you as much as it does me."

"What is it, Russell?"

Russell focused his gaze on Jonah. "Have you formed an interest in a young lady, Jonah?" he asked.

Jonah smiled, then chuckled. "No, Russell. I have not found anyone I wish to marry. In fact, marriage is the furthest thing from my mind."

"Don't you think it's time you considered finding a wife and settling down? You're not getting any younger."

"Perhaps not, Russell. But I'm not sure I wish to marry. Perhaps I'm not the marrying type. I'm perfectly content with my work, you see. I'm not sure I have time to marry."

"Then I would like to encourage you to consider it."

"You're suggesting I consider finding a wife and marrying."

"Yes," Russell said firmly.

The first stirrings of concern clutched at Jonah's insides. It was the concern he felt when he had to tell a patient that their condition was severe. "What's wrong, Russell? Are you ill?"

Russell rose and paced the floor. "No, I am not ill." He finished the brandy in his glass. "It's Julia."

"Julia? She's ill?"

"Not ill, exactly."

"Then what?"

"When she presented me with our last child, baby Rosalind, the doctor had a serious conversation with me."

"About what?"

"The state of Julia's health. My wife has always desired a large family. She wanted many children. At least six, she teased me. Three boys and three girls. But as you can see, we have only had daughters. And although I love them dearly and wouldn't trade them for anything in the world, the doctor told me if Julia risked having another child, it's likely she would not survive the pregnancy."

"What reason did he give you for making such a prediction?"

"He said he doubted her heart was strong enough to survive going through the process of birthing another child."

"I see," Jonah said softly.

"I can't take the chance, Jonah. I couldn't survive without her. I couldn't."

The terrified look on his brother's face froze Jonah where he stood.

"There are ways to prevent a pregnancy, Russell."

"I know about such ways, Jonah. Perhaps ways even you are not aware of," Russell said with reddened cheeks. "Although perhaps not. You are a doctor, after all. Keeping Julia from becoming pregnant is not all I am concerned over, however."

"Then what is it?"

"The Darbringth line. Without an heir, the Darbringth line ceases to exist. Unless you provide the next heir."

Jonah stared at his brother as if he'd lost his mind. "Is there no one else that can be named as the Darbringth heir? A distant cousin somewhere that can be named?"

"There is only one," Russell answered hesitantly.

"Who might that be?"

"Father's cousin, Rupert Reynolds. Did Father ever talk to you about him?"

"He didn't have to tell me about that reprobate," Jonah said. "I was still at home when Cousin Rupert called on Father to demand a portion of Darbringth land. He claimed he was a rightful heir to a portion of the holdings and expected Father to hand over Darland Estate. I recall vividly how ferociously they argued that day. I was afraid Father was going to be injured. Cousin Rupert was nearly twice as large as Father, and his temper was frightening."

"Mother said that you stepped in and protected Father."

"Well, someone had to. Father had been recovering from what I now believe was a heart ailment and didn't need the stress Cousin Rupert was causing."

"If something were to happen to me, I fear for Julia," Russell said. "Cousin Rupert would swoop down to demand a portion of the Darbringth holdings, and she would be no match for the pressure he would put on her."

Jonah rose from his chair and refilled his glass with brandy. "Is this why you wrote to me? Why you wanted me to return?"

"I'd be lying if I said it wasn't part of the reason. But it was not the main reason, Jonah. We've been strangers too long. You are the only family I have, and I wanted us to be closer, the same as we were at one time."

Jonah nodded. "Until Father demanded I give up my dream of becoming a doctor, or leave and never return."

"That was very unfair of him. Everyone who knew you realized how desperately you wanted to be a physician."

"Everyone but Father."

"Do you ever regret your choice?" Russell asked.

"Not for a moment," Jonah answered. "I run my own hospital now and cure patients dependent on opium. The joy I see when patients are cured of their dependence is more gratifying than anything I can describe. The families torn apart by a son or daughter's obsessive use of opium or laudanum is hard to watch. If I can heal even one family, it's worth everything I have had to give up."

Russell looked at him with a genuine expression of admiration on his face. "I envy you. You have accomplished more in your life than I can ever hope to accomplish. You have done more good than all the members of the *ton* put together."

"I wouldn't go that far," Jonah said. "But I'm glad you don't share Father's opinion regarding what I've chosen to do with my life."

"Don't ever think that I do," Russell said. "I couldn't be more proud of you."

Jonah took a swallow of his brandy. "This doesn't answer what your intentions for me are. If you don't expect Julia to provide you with more children, are you suggesting that the duty of providing a Darbringth heir is now mine?"

"That's exactly what I'm suggesting. If you can't bring yourself to marry someone who is willing to provide you with an heir or two, then we must accustom ourselves to the realization that the Darbringth line will pass down to cousin Rupert, then to his worthless son, Bradley."

Jonah considered his brother's words. Family had never meant as much to him as it had to their father or Russell. But that did not mean he didn't care about protecting the line of progeny.

He cared a great deal.

"How do you expect me to go about procuring a wife, brother?" he asked. "I've not been in London for more than ten years. I'm not even acquainted with any of the single ladies of the *ton*."

"You have all Season to work on that, Jonah. I'm sure you can find someone to marry by the end of it."

Jonah raked his fingers through his hair. He wasn't sure he could do this. He'd grown accustomed to living on his own. Accustomed to concentrating on his work, on his hospital. He wasn't sure he had it in him to care for a wife. Or learn to love her.

"You will have time, Jonah. All Season, in fact. Julia and I will show you around, and introduce you to more females to choose from than you'll be able to remember."

Jonah smiled, but that was only a reaction to hide the fear that had tightened the knot in his stomach.

"Once Julia knows you've come to find a wife," Russell said, "she will be relentless in her pursuit of the perfect female for you."

Just then, the door opened and Julia walked into the room to announce that dinner was ready. She stepped up to Jonah and held out her arm.

"We are going to have to feed you properly, Jonah. You look like your life of bachelorhood has forced you to miss too many meals. That will be first on my list of things to do for you. You must build up your strength if you are going to keep up with us and our busy schedule of attending balls and other social events. Who knows, you might even meet a female who strikes your fancy."

"That's just what we were discussing," Russell said, stepping to his wife's other side and looping her arm through his. "You'll know just the females he might find engaging."

He and his wife shared a look that told Jonah he was in more trouble than he'd ever been in his whole life. He wasn't sure he wanted to marry. It would take a special woman willing to put up with the work he did, as well as the hours of work he demanded of himself. It would take a very special woman who would be satisfied to move from London and spend her days in the country.

He doubted he could find a woman who fit those requirements. Ever.

CHAPTER TWO

J ONAH RODE IN the carriage with Russell and Julia. They were on their way to the Micklereed ball. This was the first ball he had attended in more than ten years, and to say he wasn't nervous would be a lie.

Not only could he barely recall how to behave when surrounded by members of the *ton*, he wasn't sure he remembered any of the dance steps he'd once known. He definitely didn't know the newer dance steps, and the waltz completely eluded him.

"I'm not sure I'll be able to remember how to dance," he admitted when the carriage came to a halt and a footman opened the door to allow them to exit.

"You only need to ask a lady to partner you when the orchestra is playing a dance you remember," Russell said, taking Julia by the arm and leading her to the brightly lit townhouse.

Jonah followed, trying to ignore the wild beating of his heart as they entered the elegant foyer.

"Come, Jonah," Russell said, leading the way to the ballroom. "Allow me to introduce you to Lord and Lady Micklereed. Her ladyship will consider it quite a coup that you've chosen to make your return to Society at her ball."

Jonah stood at Russell's side as their names were announced. The crowd quieted, and the throng of attendees turned to focus on Jonah.

"Well, brother, your presence has caused quite a stir," Russell whispered as they made their way down the steps to greet Lord and Lady Micklereed.

"Especially with the female members of the crowd," Julia said with a smile.

"I anticipate you won't have any trouble attracting candidates to partner with," he teased, then stopped before Lord and Lady Micklereed.

Russell made the introductions, and after Jonah greeted his host and hostess, he turned to make his way into the ballroom. His breath caught when he saw the massive crowd of onlookers staring at him. His feet nearly tripped him up.

"That's what you get for being so bloody good-looking," Russell said as he came alongside him and led him to the edge of the ballroom floor. "Every single female looking for a potential husband has her eyes on you. Even some who are just looking for some entertainment."

"I wish you had warned me there were so many vultures in Society," Jonah said as he reached for a glass from a passing footman's tray.

"And then there are the mamas who are searching for husbands for their daughters," Julia said, taking the glass Russell handed her.

"Come along, Jonah," Russell said. "Let's tour the room. With a crowd like this, it will no doubt take us most of the evening just to introduce you to anyone worth knowing."

Jonah followed Russell as they made their way around the ballroom. He recognized some of the people his brother introduced, but most he didn't. He hadn't spent enough time in Society to be able to put names with faces. Plus, he'd been absent so long that the names he *did* recognize belonged to people who didn't look at all like he thought they should. He wondered if age had changed his own appearance so dramatically. He was sure it had.

After what seemed an eternity, Russell paused. "The orchestra is playing the dinner dance. When it's finished, we'll go in to eat. I'm starving," he said, "and Lady Micklereed is known for providing a lavish spread."

Jonah looked around the room and realized he'd barely met half the guests so far. "I'm not sure I've got much of an appetite," he said.

"Coward. Come with me." Russell chuckled. "Your hunger will return once you see the food on the buffet tables. But before we go in to eat, there's one more person I want you to meet."

Jonah didn't have an opportunity to respond before Russell led him past the standing guests. He stopped before a single female who sat in a chair against the wall. A female that Society would call a wallflower.

"Dr. Reynolds, I'd like to introduce you to a longtime friend of our family."

Jonah looked at the woman before him and knew she seemed familiar. Her face opened to a bright smile, and her eyes gleamed as if she recognized him at first glance.

He tried to place her but found it difficult. She was very striking indeed, with hair a rich auburn and eyes a dark brown that seemed able to see deep inside him. She wasn't young, perhaps four or five and twenty—an age where most of Society would consider her to be on the shelf. But there was something about her that fascinated him. Something he couldn't explain, yet found mesmerizing.

"You're struggling to place me, aren't you, Jonah?" she said with a lilt to her voice. "I'll take that as a compliment. That means I've changed from the bothersome brat who used to tag along after you and my brother."

"Mariah?" he said, reaching for the dark-haired beauty's hands and raising them to his lips. "This is indeed a pleasure. You're one of the few familiar people I've met tonight."

"That's because you've avoided us for, what? It's been more than ten years, hasn't it?"

"Yes. Nearly twelve."

Jonah studied the female he'd grown up with and thought what a beauty she'd become. Her hair was darker than he remembered and her eyes were in some ways less bright, more guarded. When she was younger, they had seemed too large for her delicate features. Now her face had grown to a perfect size to make her lovely brown eyes a thing of beauty. And her lashes were so long that when she lowered her gaze, they rested on her cheeks.

The only complaint he could make about her was the outdated, unflattering gown she wore. It was almost what he'd consider dowdy, and the color did not suit her at all. She had an exquisite figure, but the style she wore hid her most flattering features. It was as if she was intentionally trying not to appear appealing. Trying not to draw attention to herself. Jonah wondered why.

"I should be angry with you, Jonah," she said, "but Lady Darbringth fills me in with the few bits of news she hears about you, which isn't much."

"Well, that is more than I hear about you, Mariah. Or does Charles still call you Mari?"

"Yes, he still calls me Mari. And I call him Charlie, except when I'm angry with him, or we're in public. Then he's Charles."

Jonah laughed at their childhood nicknames. "Do you still ride?"

Mariah's eyes lowered and her face paled. "Not as much as I used to."

Before he could consider what her reaction implied, Julia interrupted them.

"The waltz is ending, Russell," she said. "We should go in to the dining room before we have to search for a place where we can all sit together."

"You're right, sweetheart. Come, Jonah." Russell turned his attention to Mariah. "May we entice you to eat with us, Mariah?"

"I'd be delighted."

Jonah extended his arm for Mariah to take and followed Russell and Julia in to the dining room. Thankfully, not many were seated yet, and they found a table for four where they could be alone and easily converse.

"Would you like me to fill a plate, or would you rather choose your own food?" Jonah asked Mariah.

"Please, surprise me. I'm not a picky eater. Just don't get me too much. I'm not all that hungry."

"Very well," he said, then followed Russell to the buffet tables.

"I didn't even ask," he said to his brother as they each filled two plates. "Is Mariah married? Should we have saved a place at the table for her husband?"

"No, she has never married. Although I can't understand why some young man hasn't snatched her for his wife by now. It isn't that she's not gorgeous enough to catch a man's eye."

"Has she ever been rumored to be serious about anyone in particular?" Jonah asked.

"No. Never."

Jonah filed that bit of information away for further consideration. "I noticed she hasn't danced even once," he said when he'd filled both plates.

"She never does."

Jonah looked at Russell with a confused expression. "Why is she here, then?"

"She brings her sister, who is enjoying her second Season."

"Oh, I forgot there was a younger sister."

"Yes, Felicity. That's her over there," Russell said, nodding toward the couple coming through the door. "She's been seen all Season with the Earl of Pembleton. Rumor has it he's about to ask for her hand."

"I see. Yes, they make a handsome couple."

Jonah carried his and Mariah's plates and followed Russell back to the table.

"See, Mariah," Julia said, glancing at the plates of food Russell and Jonah had in their hands. "I told you the men would bring us far too much to eat."

The women laughed when the men set heaping plates in front of them.

"You realize you're going to have to help me eat all this, don't you, Russell?" she asked.

"That won't be too much of a hardship," Russell answered.

"As will you," Mariah teased Jonah.

"With pleasure," Jonah answered. "As long as you leave me some of the sweet potatoes and ham."

"Oh, those are my favorites." Her delight exposed a merry dimple in one cheek. "I'd planned on eating all of those and sending you back for heaps more."

"You're cruel," Jonah said, and his theatrically pained expression caused everyone to laugh.

"So, tell me what you've done since you've been away," Mariah said. "Julia mentioned that you've become a physician."

He took a sip of punch from his glass. "Yes, I studied to become a physician."

"Jonah runs his own hospital," Julia interjected.

"You own a hospital?"

He looked at Mariah and nodded. "I converted an abandoned convent to a hospital. We have twelve rooms dedicated to the treatment and cure of patients suffering from opium dependency."

Her hand paused in midair. "You cure people with a dependence on opium and laudanum?"

Jonah couldn't help but notice how Mariah's face paled at their discussion. He hated to think that this lovely woman thought his work had no merit.

"I know it doesn't sound like a glamorous occupation, but there is a great need for physicians who can help both men and women who have become dependent on the opium derivative. It has destroyed many a healthy person and ruined many families."

"Oh my no, I don't mean to denigrate it at all," Mariah said. "I think it's an admirable pursuit. So many families have seen their lives changed for the worse because of the drug. Are you seeing any kind of successful recovery in the people you treat?"

"Yes, our success rate is quite satisfying. Especially in those patients who are serious about being cured."

"How remarkable. Is this hospital in London?" she asked.

Jonah shook his head. "No. It's north of London, about thirty miles."

"Do you have many patients?"

He nodded. "And a waiting list of patients desperate for treatment. They come from all over. Several of our patients have come down from Scotland."

"That is quite impressive, Jonah."

Jonah stared at the inquisitive expression on Mariah's face and wondered what connection she had to someone who had a dependency on the drug. He was sure that *she* wasn't the connection. He'd become quite adept at spotting users of the drug, and Mariah didn't show any signs of being dependent on opium.

"As you can tell, I can talk about my hospital for hours," he said. "I sometimes forget that I'm the only one with such an interest, and I end up boring my listeners."

"I am not bored at all," Mariah said. "But your brother looks as though he has something he wishes to tell us. Am I right, my lord?"

"Was I that obvious?" Russell asked.

"Yes." Julia laughed.

"Then I apologize. But look. See there?" He pointed to a far table. "I notice that Lord Pembleton is with your sister again. Is their friendship becoming serious?"

"Yes, I believe it is," Mariah replied. "At least, that's the impression our family has. Charles told me as we were getting ready to leave the house tonight that Pembleton asked to speak with him tomorrow. He wanted my opinion on the matter."

"What did you say, Mariah?" Julia asked with excitement.

"I said I had no objections, and I know Felicity doesn't either."

"Oh, how exciting," Julia said. "Next, you'll be planning a wedding."

"Yes," Mariah answered.

"Will you still come to London for the Seasons after your sister marries?" Julia asked.

"No. There will be no need. I don't enjoy the city much. I greatly prefer the country. I always have."

"One or two weeks of balls and soirees and large functions is about all that I can take," Julia agreed. "Then I yearn for the peace and quiet of the country."

"What about you, Jonah?" Mariah asked. "Are you enjoying your time in London?"

"Actually, tonight is the first ball I've attended in the twelve years I've been gone. It's quite overwhelming, if I'm honest."

"I know what you mean," Mariah answered sympathetically. "I hadn't attended any large functions until Felicity had her come-out last year and I was forced to come with her. I remember how stunned and overcome I was."

"You didn't have a come-out?" Julia asked.

"No," Mariah said quietly. She then switched topics to compare what functions Felicity was planning to attend in the upcoming weeks until Russell interrupted them.

"Please, excuse me," he said, reaching for his wife's hand. "But the orchestra is about to start the next set, and I would like to dance with my wife. You and Lady Mariah are welcome to finish eating, or, if you prefer, you can join us on the dance floor."

Jonah looked at his brother. "You and Julia go ahead. We'll join you later."

"Very well," Russell said, then escorted his wife out of the emptying dining room and to the ballroom.

"I hope you don't mind staying behind, my lady," Jonah said. "I'm out of practice when it comes to dancing. But I'd be happy to escort you back to the ballroom so you can make yourself available to dance with the many men who are waiting to partner you."

"That's not necessary, Jonah. I don't care to dance."

He couldn't hide the questioning expression from his face. "May I ask why? I would think you would not lack for dance partners."

"Except that I do not want dance partners. That would give people the wrong impression."

"And what impression would that be?" he asked.

"That I was putting myself on the Marriage Mart."

"Are you saying you are not?"

"No, I am not. I have no intention of searching for a husband."

"May I ask why? Have you no intention of marrying?"

Mariah's cheeks flushed and she lowered her gaze. She slowly folded her napkin, then placed it by her plate. She looked up with a surprised expression on her face. "I see my sister and Lord Pembleton have finished eating and have returned to the ballroom. I'd best join them."

Jonah stood and extended his arm for Mariah to take. She rose gracefully and he escorted her to the ballroom.

"Did your brother accompany you tonight?" he asked.

"Yes. He's probably in the card room. I continually tell him he's not likely to meet many pretty females in the card room, but so far he hasn't taken my advice."

Jonah laughed and saw the first real smile appear on Mariah's face. "Would you care to take a turn around the room?"

For some reason he couldn't explain, he wasn't ready to leave her side. He happened to enjoy Mariah's company too much to separate himself from her. He was shocked by how much she'd changed in the twelve years since he'd last seen her. She was a very calming influence on him.

"Would you mind if we took a walk onto the terrace?" she asked. "Or perhaps through the garden?"

"Excellent idea," Jonah said, then looped Mariah's arm through his and walked in the direction of the open French doors that led onto the terrace. When they reached the outside, he led her down the three steps and onto the path that would take them through the garden. Ahead of them stood a wrought-iron bench that overlooked a small pond stocked with geese and ducks.

The two walked down the pebbled path, then followed it as it circled back. Along the way, they passed another wrought-iron bench that overlooked the opposite side of the same pond they'd passed before.

"Would you mind if we sat for a while?" Mariah asked.

"Of course not."

Jonah led Mariah to the bench and helped her sit, then sat beside her.

"I hope you don't mind, but I have to confess that I have led you out here under false pretenses," she said.

He smiled. "Ah, my lady. That sounds intriguing."

Mariah returned his smile. "Yes, I suppose it does. But it's not all that intriguing. I was fascinated with your discussion earlier concerning your hospital and wanted to hear more about it."

"Actually, it's called Hope's House."

"What a unique name. And how appropriate. Hope's House."

"I wish I could take credit for the name, but I have to share it."

"With whom?"

"With Lady Annalise Washburn. Her husband is a good friend of mine and owns the estate where Hope's House is located."

"Was there a reason Lady Annalise had such an interest in working with you to start a hospital?"

"Yes," Jonah said. "A very personal reason. Through no fault of her own, she had become an opium user and wanted to be cured."

"And did you?"

"I showed her how it was possible not to be dependent on the opiate. She did the hard work." He studied Mariah's serious expression. "Is there a reason you're asking these questions,

Mariah?"

She was about to answer when the sound of footsteps on the pathway stopped her.

"Mariah?" the deep voice interrupted. "Are you all right?"

"Oh, yes, Charles. I am very fine. Come, let me introduce you to an old friend."

A tall, good-looking young man approached them and stopped in front of them. Jonah got to his feet and smiled a broad grin. It may have been more than twelve years since they'd last seen each other, but Jonah would recognize the Earl of Aspen anywhere. "Lord Aspen."

"Jonah!" his old friend exclaimed, and wrapped his arms around him in a welcoming acknowledgment.

Jonah returned the hug, trying not to reveal what he'd just discovered. Based upon the telltale signs, Jonah recognized Mariah's brother as the reason for her intense interest in his hospital's mission. It was apparent to him that she loved her brother very much. And equally apparent that the man was in a great deal of trouble.

CHAPTER THREE

"W ERE YOU WORRIED about me, Charles?" Mariah asked in a teasing voice.

"Actually, I was excited for you, Mari," her brother replied. "When I asked Felicity if she'd seen you, she said she noticed you going to the garden with a very handsome young man. I tried to imagine who had caught your eye, but would never have guessed that it was our old friend Jonah Reynolds. Have you returned to London to stay, Jonah, or is this just a visit?"

"No, I'm not here to stay," Jonah answered. "My brother invited me to pay him a visit. He thought it was time we became reacquainted. We were separated far too long."

"Yes, we both missed you. I was sad to hear your father took the news of your desire to become a physician so negatively. Did you achieve your goal?"

"Yes, I did. I—"

"Jonah built a hospital, Charles. He's quite successful," Mariah interrupted.

For a reason Jonah understood all too well, she didn't want her brother to know exactly what Jonah did yet. Very few people with a dependency on opium felt comfortable around a physician who knew a great deal about the adverse effects the drug had on them.

"You'll have to tell me all about your work someday, Jonah,"

Charles said. "I'm anxious to hear about your accomplishments."

"I will," Jonah replied. "But now is not the time. We have too much to catch up on, and I want to hear how you're doing. My condolences on your father's passing."

"Thank you," Lord Aspen answered before his gaze wandered, which was quite normal for someone under the influence.

"How is your mother faring?"

When Charles didn't answer immediately, Mariah stepped in to cover for his lack of concentration. This seemed to be something she was used to doing.

"She misses Papa terribly, but she's getting better. We can usually talk her into joining us, but she wasn't feeling well tonight and decided to stay home."

"I hope it's nothing serious," Jonah said.

"No, nothing serious," Mariah answered. "She just preferred to stay in rather than going out."

"I understand," he said. "Tell her I missed seeing her and that it will be wonderful to see her soon."

"She'll be sorry she missed you. You'll have to call on her. Are you free tomorrow?"

"I am. I'd love to call on her."

"Wonderful," Mariah said.

"I will see you tomorrow, then, Jonah," Charles said, and slowly took a step toward the house.

"Where are you going, Charles?" she asked.

"I'm going to return to the ball," he answered.

"Have you eaten?"

"Yes, Mari. Lady Micklereed set out her usual spread that I can never pass up."

Jonah looked at the questioning expression on Mariah's face and knew she doubted her brother was telling the truth. People under the influence were seldom hungry.

"Don't go far, Charles. We will want to leave shortly."

"Is Felicity here tonight?"

"Yes, Charles. She's spent a great deal of time with Lord

Pembleton this evening. I think their attraction is escalating."

"Surely Mother won't allow Felicity to develop an attachment to Pembleton," he said. "She isn't old enough to entertain thoughts of marriage."

"Yes, she is, Charles. This is her second Season. Don't you remember?"

He looked at his sister as if she'd said something impossible. Jonah knew the normal reaction for someone under the influence was either to respond in anger or to make light of their misunderstanding. From the expression on Charles's face, Jonah was concerned that his friend would react in anger to his sister's correction.

Suddenly, he was afraid for Mariah.

"I have some friends I need to speak with before we leave," Charles said, avoiding the anger Jonah expected to rear its ugly head. As if he thought better of his reaction, he bade Jonah good evening with a promise that he'd see him tomorrow.

Jonah watched Charles shuffle down the garden path, then cross the terrace and return to the ballroom.

"Are you all right?" he asked Mariah when they were alone.

"Of course. Why wouldn't I be?"

"I'm an expert in my area, Mariah. I recognize the signs—"

"Might we walk for a while?"

"Of course, Mariah." He held out his hand for her to rise, looped her hand through his arm, and moved along the path again.

Thanks to the full moon, he was aware of her flushed cheeks and the embarrassment on her face.

"We will talk about this later. Not right now."

"Of course," Jonah said, allowing his shoulder to touch hers before they walked on in silence. Finally, they reached the end of the garden, and he followed the bend that returned them to the house.

"You know what's wrong with Charles," Mariah whispered just loud enough to be heard. "Don't you?"

"Yes. I've seen that same reaction numerous times. How long has he been using…?"

"Since he was twenty. He was in a horse-riding accident and was severely injured."

"I must have already been gone."

"Yes. You and your father had already argued over the notion that you wanted to become a doctor."

"I'm sorry I wasn't here for you, Mariah."

"So was I. More so because of Charles. He desperately needed a friend, and you were closer to him than anyone. Besides, Russell left for school shortly after the accident and was gone."

"What happened?"

"Charles jumped a hedgerow and his horse stumbled. He broke several bones in his body and nearly died. He was in a great deal of pain."

"And the doctor gave him laudanum to ease the pain," Jonah finished for her.

"No." Mariah took a deep breath. "I did."

Jonah stopped on the garden path and turned to face Mariah.

"I couldn't stand to see Charlie in so much pain. I sat with him every night, and at first I only gave him a small amount when he woke in pain. Then he needed more. And more. And more. Until the day came when he couldn't get along without it."

Jonah wrapped his arm around Mariah's shoulder and held her close. "You didn't know, Mari. You were so young. You were only what? Fifteen?"

"Sixteen," she responded. "I was sixteen and Charlie was twenty. That was a little more than ten years ago. I ruined at least ten years of Charlie's life. Ten years of Charlie getting to know Father. Ten years of Father teaching him how to be the future Earl of Aspen. How to take over what Father would leave him when he was gone."

"You can't blame yourself, Mariah. You didn't know. No one knew how much damage the drug would do."

"I should have. I could see what it was doing to Charlie, but by the time I realized the harmful effect it had on him, it was too late."

They continued their silent walk along the garden path.

"What do you want me to do, Mariah? How can I help you?" Jonah asked at last.

"Can you cure Charlie? Do you know how?"

He took a deep breath. "Yes, I know how, but I can only cure Charlie if he wants to be cured. If there's anything I've learned, it's that it takes a great amount of willpower and determination to be released from the opiate's grasp."

"Will you talk to Charlie?"

"Yes. I'll talk to him. But I'm not sure he'll listen to me."

"We won't know until we try, will we?"

He smiled. "No, we won't."

"Thank you, Jonah," Mariah said. Her eyes filled with tears as she leaned on her tiptoes and kissed Jonah's cheek.

Something awakened inside Jonah. Something he hadn't expected. He lowered his head and pressed his lips to hers.

He didn't anticipate such a tumultuous reaction from their kiss. Not the earth-shattering response that caused his heart to thunder like stampeding horses. Not the turbulent emotions that raced through his chest. Not the riotous sensations that caused every nerve in his body to explode with a passion he'd never felt before.

He lifted his lips from hers and broke their kiss. He wasn't sure why he'd kissed her. He only knew he could never kiss her again. Not unless he intended to offer for her. Because he would never be satisfied with just kissing her.

He'd want a whole lot more.

MARIAH STRUGGLED TO fall asleep. She'd returned from the Micklereed ball hours earlier, and yet sleep eluded her. Now it would be dawn soon, and all she could think about was the kiss she and Jonah had shared. Not the innocent kiss she'd pressed to his cheek, but the shattering kiss he'd given her after that. It was the first real kiss she'd ever received in her life. And it was from the last person she should ever have allowed to kiss her. Worse, it was a massively reckless move.

She and Jonah had grown up together. They'd been neighbors, lived next to each other their entire lives. And he'd never kissed her before. He'd never even *hinted* that he wanted to kiss her. But tonight he'd kissed her like he'd wanted to do that very thing his entire life. That, and more.

Why had she allowed him that sweet indiscretion? It was the last thing she should have let him do. He'd ruined everything. As long as she hadn't known what his kisses were like, she could survive never knowing what she was missing. But now she knew. And she didn't know how she would survive never experiencing that glorious wonder again.

Mariah threw the covers from her and got out of bed. She paced the floor, from one side of the room to the other, wondering what had made him do something so careless. What had caused him to do something so irresponsible.

But it was her fault. Not his.

Why had she kissed him on the cheek? She'd let her guard down and allowed him to think she was in the market for a husband. She should have found an opportunity to explain to him that she had no intention of ever marrying. That finding a husband and having a family was something she could never consider. She had no right to let him think otherwise. The kiss was all her fault, and she had to fix her mistake.

Suddenly, she needed to escape her four bedroom walls. She needed to go someplace where she could think.

Mariah threw her robe around her shoulders and left her room. She needed something to calm her nerves. She needed a cup of chamomile.

She made her way down the stairs and to the kitchen. Cook

always kept a kettle of water on the fire in case someone required something during the night, and Mariah made herself a cup of tea.

"Couldn't you sleep?" Charles asked from behind her.

"Oh," she said with a start. "You surprised me."

He sat at the kitchen table with a glass of wine in his hands.

"What are you doing awake at this hour?" she asked.

"Thinking."

Mariah prepared her cup and sat down across from Charles. "What are you thinking about?"

"Father. And how disappointed he would be with me if he knew what I've turned into."

"Don't, Charlie. Father would not be disappointed in you. He was always very proud of you. And you are only what I turned you into."

"No, Mari. You can't blame yourself for this."

She reached for Charles's hand and clasped his fingers. "The accident was my fault. No one's fault but mine. No matter how hard I try to explain it away, it was still my fault. And that's not the only thing that was my fault."

"What do you blame yourself for other than the accident? The laudanum? You didn't do anything but try to help me through the pain."

"I made you dependent on opium. I was too weak to see you in so much pain, so I gave you enough laudanum that you became dependent on it. I didn't realize the damage it would cause."

Charles looked down at the glass of wine sitting in front of him.

"Is that why you think Papa would be disappointed in you, Charlie?"

"You know he would, Mari."

"Do you think he knew?"

He nodded. "He had to have known. How could he not?"

"Sometimes, parents only see what they want to see. They can be quite blind to the things in their children that they don't want to face."

"How did you get so intelligent?"

"I learned from you."

Charles smiled, but it was a faux smile.

She gave her brother's hand a gentle squeeze, then rose from the table and poured herself another cup of chamomile. "Charlie?" she asked without turning to face him. "Would you ever want to be rid of your dependence on the opium?"

She waited for Charles's answer, but he was eerily silent. Finally, she turned to face her brother. His gaze locked with hers, and Mariah was left with no choice but to cross back to the table and sit down.

"You know that's not possible, Mari. Have you ever heard of anyone who got over their need for the drug?"

"Yes, I have."

He straightened in his chair. "What?"

"Yes, I have. I know someone who is quite successful at curing people in...in that situation."

"Who?"

"First, let me ask you why you want to quit using the drug."

"What do you mean, why do I want to quit? Because it's ruining my life. I can't sleep. I can't think. Half the time I don't even know what's going on around me. And I can't remember what I'm supposed to do."

Charles tried to pull his hand out from beneath hers, but Mariah wouldn't release her grasp.

"I was all right as long as Father was here to check what I'd done. To make sure that I'd taken adequate care of the estates and the tenants. But since he's been gone, I've let things slide that he never would have. And..."

"And what?"

"You're not going to believe this, Mari, but I'm almost thirty."

"I believe it, Charlie. I'm six and twenty." Mariah laughed, and Charles joined her.

"What I'm saying is that it's time I settled down, found a wife, thought about an heir," he said.

"Have you met someone?"

"I may have. But what decent female would consider marrying a man who can't go through a day without opium?"

"Not many, Charlie. And being dependent on opium isn't something you can hide from someone who lives with you twenty-four hours a day."

"Like a wife?"

"Yes. Like a wife."

Charles was silent while he thought about what she'd said. Then he started asking questions.

"Do you really know someone who can help me?"

"Yes. Someone who is very good at what he does."

"Who?"

"That doesn't matter just yet. What's more important is that you understand this won't be easy."

"How do you know?" he asked.

"I just do. You must want it more than you've ever wanted anything in your life."

"I do, Mari. I do."

"Then I'll help you."

CHAPTER FOUR

"**D**O YOU HAVE plans for tonight?" Russell asked Jonah as they ate breakfast.

Jonah paused as he spread jam on his toasted bread. He'd been in London a week now and had been on the go the entire time.

Russell and Julia had made sure he was in attendance at every event Society hosted. He'd attended more balls, soirees, afternoon teas, and dinners than he thought it was possible for Society to fit into one week.

He'd danced with more females than he thought populated the *ton*, and had lost count of the number of toes he'd stepped on. He'd had conversations with every available female Russell or Julia thought he might be attracted to and hadn't found one that stirred his interest.

Except for one. Mariah.

Now, he silently hoped that whatever was going on tonight was something he could excuse himself from. He was desperate for some time alone. He needed to think.

"Is something important going on?" he asked.

"I was going to take Julia to the opera," his brother replied. "Would you like to join us?"

Jonah thought for several moments. It had been years since he'd last attended the opera, and it was something he'd always enjoyed, but tonight he would find it more appealing just to stay home.

"As much as I'd enjoy going with you, I think I'll just stay home and enjoy a night of peace and quiet. Besides, I've tagged along with you and Julia everywhere you've gone since I arrived. I'm sure you'd like some time alone with your wife."

Russell smiled. "I never refuse time alone with my wife. Thankfully, she enjoys my company as well as I enjoy hers."

"Then I'll let you appreciate your evening together."

At that moment, Julia entered the room. "Have we made you feel that you're intruding?" she asked from the doorway. "If we have—"

"No, Julia. Not at all."

She looked at him like she was trying to make sure Jonah was telling the truth.

"Truly, Julia," he assured her. "I would simply like a quiet evening. It's more what I'm used to."

"If you're sure," she said. "Because you're more than welcome to join us."

Jonah and Russell stood, and Russell slid Julia's chair out for her to sit. He filled her a plate and set it down in front of her.

"I know I am," Jonah told her. "But I haven't given you and Russell an evening to yourselves since I arrived. Nor have I had any time to myself."

"Then you stay in tonight and get rested up," she replied.

"That's exactly what I intend to do," he said as a footman entered the room with a missive on a silver tray.

"A message for Dr. Reynolds, my lord."

Jonah took the message from the tray and opened it. He read it carefully, then folded it. "It's an invitation from Lord Aspen and his sister. They've invited me to dine with them tonight. I guess I won't stay in tonight after all."

"I guess you won't," Russell said.

"You are among a select few who have been chosen to dine with Charles and Mariah," Julia said. "I can't remember the last time Lord Aspen and his sister entertained guests."

"We grew up together and were close friends, weren't we, Russell?"

"Yes. You were more Aspen's age, so were closer friends than I was. And I hate to admit it, but I haven't associated much with him since his father died."

"Is there a reason?"

"Nothing in particular," Russell answered. "It's only that Charles has become unapproachable since he ascended to the earldom. Especially after the accident."

"What accident?"

Mariah had mentioned the accident and blamed herself for her brother's use of opium. But Jonah was interested to hear if Russell had more information.

"It was a riding accident, if I remember correctly. It happened shortly after you left."

"I see. Was he severely injured?"

"I couldn't really tell you. I had left for university shortly before it happened."

"Well, maybe I'll ask tonight."

"I'm sure you'll enjoy yourself, Jonah," Julia said.

"I'm sure I will. I'm looking forward to the evening."

"Then I won't worry about you, brother," Russell said. "Perhaps you've already formed an attachment with Aspen's sister. Mariah is a beautiful woman. I have never figured out why she hasn't married. It isn't that she wouldn't be an admirable catch."

"Has she ever formed an attachment to anyone?" Jonah asked.

"Not that I'm aware of," Julia said. "Many suitors have vied for her hand, but she's rejected each and every one of them without allowing herself time to even get to know any of them."

"And she is rumored to have one of the largest dowries in Society, which makes her even more desirable," Russell added.

Jonah didn't care about Mariah's dowry. That wasn't important to him. The only trait he cared about was whether or not they would get along with each other. He already knew they would.

And he was more than simply fond of her. He always had been. After the kiss they shared the night before, he was almost certain she felt the same. And he knew the feelings she stirred in him could easily turn to love. If his goal was to marry and provide the heir Russell so desperately wanted, he couldn't imagine anyone better suited to be the mother of his children than Mariah. Nor could he imagine anyone else with whom he would want to spend his life.

"I'm going to take a ride through Hyde Park this morning," Russell said as they finished breakfast. "Would you care to join me?"

"I can't think of anything I'd enjoy more," Jonah said. "It's been forever since I've ridden through Hyde Park."

"Then let's go. I'll have two horses saddled for us."

The pair rose from the table. "We'll be back before lunch," Russell told his wife. "We both have big evenings planned," he said, then kissed her on the cheek as they left the room.

Jonah followed his brother from the room and walked from the townhouse with a light step. He realized he couldn't wait for evening to come. He couldn't wait to spend it with Mariah.

MARIAH SAT IN her bedroom in front of the mirror and perused her appearance. A part of her wanted to look her very best for Jonah, while another part of her wanted to look so unappealing that he wouldn't be attracted to her.

She moved to stand before the mirror and examined the gown she'd chosen to wear. It was one she'd never worn before, one that her mother insisted she have made because the style and color were prettily suited to her complexion.

She told herself she couldn't allow herself to care how she

looked in the gown, but she had to admit that she did care. Just for tonight, she wanted to look lovely for Jonah.

When she was assured she looked her best, she left her room and made her way down the stairs. In the receiving room she poured herself a small glass of wine and took a sip.

She never should have allowed Jonah to kiss her last night. She'd sworn she would never allow *anyone* to kiss her. Never allow anyone to break through the wall she'd erected around her heart. She couldn't. She had nothing to offer any man. Less than nothing.

Yet she had. She'd allowed Jonah to kiss her and would regret it for the rest of her life.

She took another sip of her wine, then sat up when Charles entered the room.

"Oh, Mari. You look delectable this evening. I'm not used to seeing you dressed up so."

"Am I too formal?"

"No, no. You're perfect." He stepped to the small table where the liquor decanters sat. "When are you going to tell me who we're expecting? You've kept our mystery guest's identity a secret since you told me you intended to invite someone to help me."

"That's because I didn't want you to form an opinion of our guest."

"Why?"

"Because I wanted it to be a surprise."

Charles smiled. "I'm sure it will be."

"Yes. No doubt."

"How did you ever talk Mother into chaperoning Felicity to the Parker ball?"

"Oh, that was easy. I told her I needed her to take my place because I was entertaining a male caller. She was so excited at the possibility that I had a suitor, she didn't hesitate to agree."

"I know that you're only doing this for me, Mari," he said.

"I'm doing this for *us*, Charles. You are the Earl of Aspen. You have responsibilities, and one of those responsibilities is to provide a future heir. Besides, I'm the one who made you what you are."

"No, you're not, Mari."

"Yes, I am. And we both know it." Mariah studied her brother. "Will you be all right tonight?"

"Yes," he answered on a sigh. "I only took a small amount of the elixir. Just enough to calm my nerves."

She smiled. "I'm so proud of you for going through with this, Charles."

"Don't give me too much credit yet, Mari. I haven't gone through anything yet."

"But you will. And you'll beat this curse."

"But you still won't tell me who our mystery guest is," he said. "Is there a reason?"

"Only a selfish one."

Charles laughed. "You've never committed a selfish act in your life, Mari. So, why have you kept our dinner guest's identity a mystery?"

Mariah hesitated. She wasn't sure she wanted to tell Charles the reason. It had sounded so rational when she first thought of it. Now, it only seemed trivial.

"If you must know, I didn't want anyone to know, especially Mama," she answered. "I was afraid you might accidentally let it slip who was coming and she'd get the wrong idea."

"And what idea would that be?"

"That I was interested in our guest for personal reasons. And I'm not."

The smile faded from Charles's face. "I see."

"Don't look so disappointed, Charles. I've told you a thousand times that I have no intention of ever marrying."

"But why? You would make some fortunate man an excellent wife and mother of his children."

"That doesn't alter the fact that I have no intention of marrying. Therefore, it's unfair to allow any gentleman to think I have an interest in him only to declare that I don't."

"So, you're telling me that you've only invited our mystery caller for my benefit."

Mariah reached out and placed her hand over her brother's. "Yes, Charles. I invited this particular guest because I trust him. I'm certain he can help you. I can't ask for anything more."

Thankfully, she heard a commotion in the foyer and waited until Jenkins announced their guest.

"Your guest has arrived," their butler said.

"Show him in, Jenkins."

She waited until Jonah entered, then watched her brother's reaction.

"Jonah," Charles said, stepping over and reaching for his friend's hand. "This is a delightful surprise."

"You didn't know I was coming?" Jonah said, then shifted his gaze to where Mariah sat.

Her cheeks warmed. "I wanted to surprise Charles. Plus, I was afraid if Mother discovered you were joining us, she would decide to stay home. Spending an evening with you would be far more enjoyable than chaperoning Felicity to another ball. And we didn't want to share you."

"How clever you are," Jonah said with a heart-stopping smile.

She tried not to react to his presence, tried to keep her heart from racing in her breast, but that was impossible to do. Jonah Reynolds was more handsome than any man had a right to be. It didn't help that she had been infatuated with him since she was a young lass and had followed him and Charles around like a love-struck puppy.

"Here, Jonah," Charles said, handing his friend a snifter of brandy. "Please, have a seat."

Jonah sat beside Mariah on the sofa, and Charles sat facing them.

"Dinner should be ready any moment now, then after we eat, I want you to explain what you do at your hospital, Jonah."

"Of course. I'm very proud of the work we do at Hope's House. I quite enjoy talking about everything we've accomplished."

"You know, then, that I have need of your help," Charles said after taking a swallow of his brandy.

"Yes. I knew you needed help when I met you that first night at the ball."

"It is that obvious?"

"To a doctor who has worked with patients under the influence of opium every day for years, yes." Jonah paused as if deciding what to ask his friend first. "How long have you been taking the drug?"

"For more than ten years," Charles said.

"It was shortly after you left home, Jonah," Mariah interjected. She didn't want Jonah to know every detail of their accident, not that Charles even knew every detail. But the less Jonah knew of her part in the awful incident, the better. "Charles was involved in a riding accident. He was severely injured. He almost died."

"I see," Jonah said.

"That's when I started giving him a few drops of laudanum in some wine."

"You must have been in a great deal of pain." Jonah looked toward Charles, who dropped his head and nodded slowly.

"Well," she continued, "it's my fault he's dependent on the drug."

"No, it's not, Mari," her brother insisted.

"Yes, it is, Charles. You know it is." Mariah shifted her gaze to Jonah. "I couldn't stand to see Charles in so much pain, so I would sneak into his room when no one was there and give him more pain medicine. I wasn't aware that the medicine actually opium and that a person could become dependent upon it. I only knew that Charles felt better when I gave it to him."

"Unfortunately, that's a common misunderstanding people have concerning opium. They're dependent on it before they realize the damage it has caused." Jonah turned his attention to Charles. "May I ask, how much of the elixir have you had tonight?"

"Only a small amount," Charles answered. "If I take too much, it slows my mind."

"That's normal," Jonah said. "And what do you consider a small amount?"

"Oh, just five or six drops," Charles said, waving his hand as though it were a minor thing.

Before they could discuss things further, Jenkins announced that dinner was served, and they all rose. Jonah extended his arm to escort her in to dinner, and Mariah instinctively placed her hand on his sleeve.

She wasn't prepared for her reaction, but every nerve in her body came alive the second she placed her hand on his arm. She lifted her head and found her gaze locked with Jonah's.

Even though she'd promised herself that she wouldn't allow Jonah to know how his nearness affected her, she knew from the intense look in his eyes that it was already too late.

CHAPTER FIVE

A FTER DINNER, MARIAH took them into the library and Charles poured two snifters of brandy and one glass of wine. He gave Mariah the wine, and after he'd given Jonah his brandy, he dismissed the staff. The door closed softly behind Jenkins, and they were alone.

"How are you feeling?" Jonah asked Charles.

"I'm starting to get...shaky."

"That's normal. What comes next?"

Charles leveled him a stern look. "You should know," he answered.

"Charles," Mariah warned.

"That's all right, Mariah," Jonah said. "Charles is fine. What comes next?"

"I start to perspire. Then I get nervous. And angry."

"Then what?"

Charles threw the liquor he had left in his snifter to the back of his throat. "I don't know. I've never been able to let myself get beyond that point."

"Then what do you do?"

"I take more of the elixir. I need it. Badly."

"Do you need to take some now?"

"Yes."

"Then add something to your glass."

"Now?"

"Yes. Going without won't do you any good right now."

Jonah didn't ask more. He waited while Charles excused himself for a few moments, then returned.

"What will happen to me next?"

"It's not going to be easy, Charles. But the good thing is that you won't remember any of it."

"Will I be alone?"

Jonah chuckled softly. "Do you want to be alone?"

"No."

"Good. Because I wouldn't allow any patient to go through the process alone. I'll be there, as well as Mariah."

She stilled. "Me?"

Jonah shifted his gaze to her. "I assumed you would want to be with Charles."

"I didn't think you would allow—"

"I've discovered that patients improve faster when someone they're close to is with them."

"Do you want me to be with you?" Mariah asked her brother.

"Of course I do," Charles said. "There isn't anyone I'd rather have with me than you."

"Very well."

"All we have to figure out then is when we're going to get you well."

"Soon," Charles answered.

"Soon it is," Jonah said. "I'll be ready to go whenever you're ready to travel."

"Travel? Can't we do it here in London?" Charles asked.

"No. I'd rather take you to Hope's House."

"The hospital?"

"Yes. It's a hospital, but we call it the house."

"How long will I be there?"

"My guess is a month. Give or take."

"Give or take what?"

"How fast you recover. I've found that the patients who

return home before they are ready revert to their old habits."

Charles rose to his feet. "I see." He took a few steps, then stopped in front of Mariah. "Can you manage this?"

"You'll have to tell Mama," she said. "We can't leave without explaining where we're going and why."

"I was hoping she'd never have to know."

"You don't think she does?" Jonah asked. "Your mother's not a fool. She's watched over you for nearly thirty years."

Mariah gave her brother a shy smile that told him Jonah was probably right.

"We'll have to ask Aunt Genevieve to come stay with Mama while we're gone," Mariah said. "She'll need help chaperoning Felicity to all the events she'll want to attend."

"Is there anything else?" Charles asked.

"Not that I can think of," she answered. "What about you?"

"I'll have to speak with my land steward and make sure he knows what to do while I'm gone, and where to get in touch with me should he need to."

"How long will it take you to get everything arranged?" Jonah asked.

Mariah locked her gaze with Charles's, and a silent understanding passed between them.

"A week," Charles answered.

"Yes, we'll be ready a week from tomorrow," she added. "Your brother will be disappointed when he finds out you're cutting your visit short."

"We'll be back before the Season is over," Jonah said. "Russell and I will still have some time together."

"Was that the only reason you came to London?" Charles asked.

Jonah wasn't prepared for Charles's question. From the expression on her face, neither was Mariah. Her head turned, and she faced Jonah with a puzzled look.

"Was there another reason?" she asked.

"Nothing important," he answered.

Charles chuckled. "That's not what the wagers in the betting book at White's are saying."

"What does that mean?" she asked. "What wagers?"

"The wagers of who Jonah will choose for his bride by the end of the Season."

Her jaw dropped. "What?"

"Everyone knows that the main reason Jonah returned to London was to find a wife," Charles said as if he were telling some huge secret. A secret he was glad he could be the first to reveal.

"Is that true, Jonah?"

"You know Russell, Mariah," Jonah replied. "He thinks I work too hard, and he assumes that there is not enough social life at Hope's House to allow me to meet enough females of a marrying age."

"And," Charles said, reaching for the decanter to refill Jonah's and his glasses, "everyone knows that Russell's wife has given him only daughters—to say nothing of the fact that she's at an age where she may or may not have any more children. Therefore, if they want to keep the Aspen title in the Reynolds family, Jonah will have to provide a male heir to preserve the title."

Mariah's face paled and her eyes opened wide. "I need to apologize, Jonah. I didn't realize you had a purpose in coming to London."

"There's no need to apologize, Mariah," Jonah said. "Helping Charles is more important than attending balls and stepping on the toes of unwitting females."

He noticed that Mariah's hand trembled when she placed her glass on the table in front of her. The subject of his searching for a wife had not occurred to her. He wasn't sure if that was a positive sign.

Jonah and Charles chatted a little while longer, and after a while Jonah was aware that the effects of the opium Charles had taken earlier were wearing off.

"I have had a wonderful evening, Charles. Thank you for

inviting me."

"Are you leaving?"

"In a few minutes. I think you have managed quite long enough before it becomes uncomfortable for you to remain."

"You understand the problems quite well," Charles said.

"I've had several years to hone my craft."

"Thank you for coming," Charles said, shaking his friend's hand. "I am so glad you were the mystery guest Mariah invited. There isn't anyone I would want to help me more than you."

"And I want you to know that I'm very proud of you. Not many who have a reliance on opium have the courage to get the help they need. You are to be congratulated."

"I owe my courage to Mari. She's the one who pushed me to do this."

"Then she is to be thanked," Jonah said, looking at Mariah.

"Good night, Mari," Charles said, then left the room.

When he was gone, Jonah lowered his head and his gaze locked with Mariah's. Her eyes were brimming with tears.

"Are you all right, Mariah?"

"Yes," she said as the first tear ran down her cheek.

He sat on the sofa close to her, wrapped his arm around her shoulders, and brought her close to him. "It will be all right, Mariah. Charles is strong. He will be fine, because you and I are here to help him."

"I know he will. He's determined to rid himself of opium. And for all the right reasons."

"Then what is it? Why are you crying?"

"I've ruined everything," she said on a sob. "I'm so sorry, Jonah."

"What are you talking about? You haven't ruined anything, Mariah."

"Yes, I have. I wish I had known, but I didn't."

"Known what?"

"That you were here in search of a wife."

"Oh, Mariah," he said, cupping her cheek in his palm. He

extended his thumb and wiped a tear from her cheek, then lowered his head and pressed his lips to hers.

JONAH WAS KISSING her.

Mariah had known she should stop him before his lips covered hers, but she couldn't. She wanted him to kiss her too badly. She wanted him to hold her too badly. She needed him to kiss her more than she'd ever needed anything before.

His kiss contained a passion unlike anything she'd experienced in her life. The feel of her body pressed to his caused a fiery heat to soar through her limbs.

"Mariah," he whispered, and she opened her mouth to respond to his plea. When her lips parted, his tongue skimmed her lips, then entered her mouth. An unexplainable, heady emotion overtook her. Every nerve in her body exploded.

He kissed her again, then deepened his kisses with a desperation that encouraged her to give everything she could to answer his pleas.

She wrapped her arms around Jonah's neck, and he tilted her head to give himself greater access to her mouth. Mariah answered his desperation with a hunger that seemed to burn within her.

Her heart raced in her chest. Her flesh shuddered wherever Jonah touched her. And still, Mariah craved more of his touches. More of his desire. More of his kisses.

She didn't want to ache for him as desperately as she did. She didn't want to lose herself to his demands, but she couldn't stop herself. She didn't want to give her heart into his care, but it was too late. He already owned her heart. She didn't only care for him. She loved him. She loved him more than she thought it was possible for her to love anyone.

If only love was possible for her. But it was an emotion she could never allow herself to experience. Especially love for a man who was searching for a wife who could give him the children he desperately needed.

Mariah turned her head and broke off their kiss. "That didn't just happen," she stated between gasps.

"Yes, it did, Mariah. And it was…shattering."

She bolted to her feet. "No! I shouldn't have allowed it to happen. It wasn't real. We can't let it be real."

"Why, Mariah?" he said, rising to his feet and closing the distance between them.

"Because you need a wife. You need someone to marry and give you children. That's not me, Jonah. That's not me!"

"That's not what your kisses tell me," he said with a smile on his face.

"Kissing you was a mistake. I shouldn't have let that happen."

"But it did."

"Don't, Jonah! Don't make this any harder than it is. You have to forget that our kiss ever happened."

"And if I can't?"

"Then I'll have to convince you that it didn't."

He chuckled. "And how are you going to do that?"

"I need you to leave, Jonah. You need to leave and never see me again."

"That will be a little difficult when we are going to spend the next month or more together."

She shook her head, then turned away from him. "No. I can't go with you."

"What are you saying, Mariah?"

"I can't go with you. Charles will find someone else to accompany him."

"But he wants you. He needs you."

"Except I can't go. It's impossible for me to go with him."

"Why? Because you can't be with me?"

"Yes! I can't risk being around you."

Jonah clasped his hands around her arms and turned her to

the sofa. "Sit down, Mariah."

She sat, and Jonah sat beside her. He reached for her hands and held them. "Very well," he said. "Tell me what's going on. What's this all about?"

She tried to keep her emotions locked inside her so they wouldn't escape, but she knew when she spoke they'd fly into the air. She lifted her gaze and focused on Jonah's face. "It's me, Jonah. I can't be what you want me to be."

"What is it you think I want you to be?"

"It doesn't matter what it is you want from me," she choked out. "I can't be anything to you."

"What are you telling me? What about the way you kissed me?"

"That was a mistake. If things were different, I might be able to offer you at least friendship. But I can't even offer you that."

"Why not?"

"Because friendship wouldn't be enough for you, Jonah. And eventually it wouldn't be enough for me either."

"Would that be so terrible?"

Mariah tried to smile, but looking at the expectant expression on his face was so painful that she felt as if her heart had shattered into a thousand pieces. "Yes, Jonah. That would be devastating."

He rose from beside her and slowly made his way to the French doors that opened onto the terrace. He opened the doors and took in several deep breaths. "Your brother needs you, Mariah."

"I know," she whispered.

He turned around and faced her. "If I promise that I won't kiss you while we're gone, or demand anything from you, will you come with Charles?"

Mariah considered his promise as well as the chance of his keeping that promise and felt her heart sink in her chest. She owed Charles. It was her fault they'd had the accident. Her fault he was dependent on laudanum. Her fault that he had to go through treatments to rid himself of the opium.

Everything was her fault. She owed Charles his life back.

Mariah slowly lifted her head. "I will hold you to your promise, Jonah. Don't expect anything from me. Especially a future."

"Do I get an explanation? Will you give me a reason you think you can offer me nothing when it's obvious you can give me everything I want?"

A sharp pain stabbed through her breast. "Someday, perhaps. Not tonight."

"Very well," he said, and turned to leave. "This isn't over, Mariah. You owe me an explanation. I deserve to know why you insist that you can't give me what I want and what I need. Especially when it's so obvious that you feel the same about me as I feel about you."

"That's the problem, Jonah. I can't. I can't," she repeated, then watched him walk from the room and from her life. The beginning of what she knew would be a lifetime of tears streamed down her cheeks.

What Charles would have to endure to rid his body of the poison that was killing him would be the hardest thing he'd ever done.

What she would have to go through if she went with him would take every ounce of her willpower. She had to swear that she would not let Jonah kiss her again.

And she could not afford to fail.

CHAPTER SIX

MARIAH SAT ON the seat beside Charles as their carriage traveled through the countryside toward Jonah's hospital. Every once in a while she reached out and placed her hand on top of Charles's to give his fingers a comforting squeeze. He answered her gesture with a tense but reassuring smile.

Jonah sat on the seat opposite them.

Today was the first time she'd seen him since the night he'd come for dinner. Since the night he'd kissed her.

He and Charles carried on a companionable conversation as they traveled. Mariah mostly remained quiet, except when Charles asked a direct question about the medical procedure and she needed some clarification on what was about to happen.

She couldn't help but be impressed. Jonah had such a calming manner that he could quickly put Charles at ease.

"We're almost there," Jonah said when he looked out the carriage window. "Before we arrive, I'd like to discuss our schedule."

"Do you intend to begin the treatment today?" Charles asked.

"Yes, if that meets with your approval."

Charles turned his head and met Mariah's gaze. She nodded.

"Yes," he answered. "Waiting will not make this any easier."

"Good," Jonah said with a smile. "We'll get you settled as soon as we arrive. I'll show you to your room first, Charles. Then

I'll show Mariah to her room. I've instructed my assistants to put her in a room close by. When you're settled, we can eat a little something before we begin."

Just then, the carriage turned up a lane and stopped in front of Jonah's hospital.

He got out first and turned to help Mariah disembark. When she was on the ground, she looked at the place that was to be her home for the next month.

"This is impressive, Jonah," she said when she took in her surroundings. "It's very beautiful."

"I'm glad you approve."

She studied the lettering above the door. *Hope's House.*

"The name is perfect, too. Everyone who comes here comes with hope for their future."

"That's exactly the purpose of Hope's House. Hope for a better future."

"That's what you're going to get, Charles," Mariah said, reaching for her brother's hand.

"Come," Jonah said. "Let me show you inside."

Mariah walked in between them and came to a halt. "Oh, Jonah. It's perfect. It's not like a hospital at all. It's like a…a resort in Bath."

"That was my intention when I planned it," he replied. "The building used to be a convent. The nuns took excellent care of it, and the design was perfectly suited for individual rooms. This staircase takes you to the rooms for our female guests. The opposite staircase leads to the rooms for our male guests. As you see, the two wings are separated by a locked gate and an employee standing guard at all times."

"So I shall be safe, then," Charles said with a wry smile. He stepped toward the stairs that led to the wing for male guests.

Jonah held up his hand to stop him. "You won't have a room with the other guests, Charles. You will have special accommodations."

Mariah and Charles looked at him.

"I promised I'd put Mariah in a room close to yours. She can't stay where the men stay."

"Of course," Mariah said.

"Follow me." Jonah motioned. "I'll show you to your rooms."

He led them down a hallway off the foyer and to a suite of rooms.

"Are these your rooms?" she asked.

"Sometimes. When they're not in use and I need to be by myself."

Mariah entered the rooms first and looked around. The first room was a sitting room. It had a floral sofa with small tables on either end, a cluster of chairs surrounding the fireplace, and a writing desk beneath a window that looked out onto a small flower garden. The blossoms were plentiful.

"It's lovely," she said.

"This is one of my favorite spots in the house."

"I can see why."

"Here, Charles." Jonah turned to the right. "This will be your room. You will notice it's not decorated as lavishly as the sitting room. That's because you will hardly recall your time spent in here. How are you feeling?"

"Like I need my elixir," Charles replied.

Jonah nodded in understanding. "That's normal. It's been a while since you've last had anything. Why don't you remove your jacket, cravat, and shoes, and make yourself comfortable while I show Mariah to her room? There should be a nightshirt on the end of the bed. Put that on and relax as much as possible. I'll send up a sandwich and something to drink."

He looked at Mariah. "Come with me," he said, and extended his hand.

She took his arm and followed him down a short hall to a second door.

"This will be your room, Mariah."

He opened the door, and she entered. "Oh, Jonah. It's lovely."

"Aren't you going to tell me it's too masculine for your tastes?"

"No. It's perfect."

The room was decorated in shades of blues and greens and yellows and browns. It was neither masculine nor feminine.

It had much of the same furnishings as the sitting room. The bed was on the far side of the room, and there was a sofa on the opposite side. Instead of a window that looked out onto the flower garden, her room had a single glass-paned door that led out into the garden. There was a small writing desk close to the fireplace that gave the room a cozy, homey appearance.

Mariah felt perfectly content in the room. She could see herself being very comfortable here.

"Thank you, Jonah. This is charming. But where are you going to sleep?"

"Oh, I thought I'd sleep on the other side of the bed, next to you."

Her terrified glare darted to meet his, and he burst out laughing.

There was a teasing glint in his eyes that she remembered from their childhood. "I wasn't serious, Mariah. I made you a promise, and I intend to keep it."

"I should have known that." Her cheeks burned with embarrassment. "I'm sorry."

"That's not a problem. Now, you settle in, and when you're ready, go through the sitting room to Charles. I'll have a light lunch sent up for you, too, and you can eat with him, although I doubt Charles will want much."

"Is this going to be difficult, Jonah?"

"I wish I could tell you it wasn't, but I can't lie to you. This is going to be the hardest thing you or Charles have ever gone through."

Mariah felt a knot form in her throat.

"You'll have to be strong, Mariah. For Charles. He'll need

your strength."

Her eyes filled with tears as she tried to steady her gaze, but she was able to nod.

He reached over and gave her fingers a gentle squeeze. "But I'll be with you, so don't worry." He turned and left the room.

Mariah wasn't sure if she could muster the strength Charles would need from her to get through this, but she didn't have a choice. She was the one who'd caused his dependency on his elixir. Now she would have to help him get free of the poison that possessed his body.

MARIAH SAT WITH Charles for several hours. She tried to convince him to eat, but he had no interest in food. Little by little, he got worse. His hands shook and he bolted to his feet several times and paced the room.

She tried to keep a conversation going, but it was difficult. Charles wasn't listening to anything she said, and instead of being comforted by the sound of her voice, he became irritated. He raised his voice and snapped at her.

"You need to leave now, Mariah," Jonah said when Charles wrapped his arms around his waist and clutched his stomach. He doubled over in pain and bellowed a vicious growl.

"I can't, Jonah. I can't leave him."

"You can't stay. It's only going to get worse."

"Oh, Jonah."

"Leave, Mariah," Jonah ordered her. "Get her out of here," he said sternly to one of the three assistants helping him restrain Charles. The man nearest her stepped close and ushered her to her own room.

"Try to get some rest, my lady," he said.

"How long will this last?"

"It's hard to say, my lady. Dr. Reynolds said that your brother has been taking laudanum for a number of years. It will take quite some time to rid his body of the poison he's been ingesting."

"How long have you been with Dr. Reynolds?"

"Since he opened Hope's House," the man replied. "I heard of his work and came to learn from him."

"Do you enjoy what you do here?"

"I can't imagine doing anything more worthwhile. Nor would I want to work with anyone other than Dr. Reynolds. He's a miracle worker. A genius."

"Yes, he seems quite knowledgeable in what he does."

"There's no one better. Your brother is in excellent hands. Now, get some rest, my lady. Tomorrow will be an even longer day."

Mariah stepped into the room and closed the door. After she'd readied herself for bed, she lay down and closed her eyes. But sleep eluded her. It was too quiet, and even though she tried to shut out Charles's moans and cries for help, it was impossible to do so completely.

She remained in bed as long as she could, and when she couldn't stand it any longer, she got to her feet, donned a robe and slippers, and left her room. She walked down the hallway until she reached Charles's room.

With each step his cries of pain grew louder, and it was impossible to ignore them. She turned the knob to her brother's room and slowly pushed the door open. What she saw tore at her heart.

Charles was out of bed, and the young assistant who had escorted her to her room gripped him around his waist. Two more assistants had his arms. When they had Charles under control, they carried him back to his bed and laid him down.

He kicked and twisted and fought them with every ounce of his strength. The vile curses that came from his mouth were so unlike her brother that she couldn't believe he even knew such words, let alone said them with such familiarity.

Mariah wrapped her arms around her waist and held herself

as if her grip could reduce the pain she was experiencing. She closed her eyes, and when they opened, she caught sight of Jonah. He stood with his hands braced against the wall and his head lowered between his outstretched arms. His shirt was soaked with perspiration and his breaths came in harsh, punishing gasps. His sleeves were rolled to his elbows and his shirt was open nearly to his waist.

Finally, he pushed himself away from the wall and reached out for the dry cloth lying on the dresser beside him. He wiped the perspiration from his face, and when he lifted his head, he saw her.

He wiped the perspiration from his neck and down the front of his open shirt then hastily buttoned it. With something akin to frustration, he stepped close to her and opened the door.

"Come with me," he said as Charles let out another agonizing moan.

When Mariah didn't immediately move, he clasped his fingers around her arm and led her from the room.

"You shouldn't be here. I didn't want you to see that," he said, leading her to the sitting room. He opened a door to a cupboard and removed a crystal decanter of brandy. He poured a generous amount into a snifter and took a liberal swallow. Then he put some wine in a glass and handed it to her.

She took it from his hand and stared into his eyes. "How do you manage to endure what your patients have to go through?"

He smiled. "How do I endure what Charles is going through?" He took another swallow of his brandy. "I endure it because I know that when my patients have rid the poison from their bodies, they will be better human beings. They will be whole again."

"Oh, Jonah," Mariah sighed, then choked back the tears that threatened to fall. "Will Charles remember any of this?"

"Very little of it. The most important thing he'll know is that he's a different person than he was when opium controlled his body and his mind. That will be a life-changing feeling. And he'll thank you for it, Mariah. Truly he will."

Just then, Charles released a loud growl, and one of the attendants guarding him yelled in pain.

"Were you holding him before I came into the room?" she asked. "Is that why you were perspiring like you were?"

"Yes," Jonah answered as he darted for the door. "Stay here. I need to check on something."

Mariah watched him race out of the room then sat on the sofa and buried her face in her hands. Tears spilled from her eyes and ran down her face. She didn't know for whom she was crying: Charles, because he was going through such hell, or Jonah, because she realized how much she loved him yet knew she couldn't dare to. Or herself, because it was her fault Charles was so dependent on opium. If only she had known how dangerous the drug was. If only she had known the lives it had destroyed.

Wracking sobs continued until Mariah had no more tears to shed. She reached for her handkerchief and wiped her cheeks, but not before Jonah stepped back into the room.

"Charles is all right, Mariah. The first few days are always the roughest."

"How long will this last?"

"There's no way to tell. It all depends on how much poison is in his body, and how long it takes to get it all out."

Jonah walked over to the sofa and sat down next to her. When he was settled, he reached for her hand and held it.

Bolts of emotions attacked her and caused her body to grow warm. There was something about being near Jonah that affected her unlike anything she'd ever felt before.

"Are you all right, Mariah?"

"I don't know," she answered. "I can't explain what it is that I'm feeling."

"I know," he said, then placed his arm around her shoulder and brought her close.

Mariah rested her head beneath his chin and listened to the

rapid beating of his heart. It was such a strong beat, and the longer she kept her cheek nestled there, the louder and faster his heart thundered beneath her ear.

She slowly lifted her head and tilted her chin upward. Her gaze locked with his, then lowered to his lips. She wanted to kiss him. She ached to feel his lips pressed against her. Ached to have his mouth open atop hers and his tongue delving inside her mouth. But if she wanted him to kiss her, she would have to instigate it.

She had forced him to promise that he wouldn't kiss her again, and she had no doubt that he would honor his word, even if it killed him to do it.

Mariah skimmed her hands up his chest and wrapped her arms around his neck, then raised her head enough that her lips were close to his.

"Mariah?"

"Jonah, I need you to kiss me."

"Are you sure?"

"I've never been more sure of anything in my life," she answered in jagged breaths.

And he lowered his head just enough that his lips were pressed to hers.

His tongue skimmed the seam of her lips, and she opened to allow him to enter. Every part of her body exploded in a fiery inferno. Mariah struggled to keep her passion under control, but it was impossible. She wanted him too desperately. She was frantic to be as close to him as possible. She desired him with a recklessness that was uncontrollable.

He deepened his kiss and demanded more from her than she thought she was able to give, but he wouldn't give up until she answered his pleas with careless abandon.

Their breathing came in harsh, ragged gasps and Mariah was afraid she would lose her ability to breathe. Just when she thought she couldn't give any more of herself, Jonah broke their contact.

He wrapped his arm around her shoulder and brought her close against him. "Mariah," he said on a gasp. "Oh, Mariah. I love you."

She tried to ignore his words but couldn't. She felt the same. What she experienced when he kissed her was beyond comprehension. It was unlike any thrill she'd ever felt before.

"Tell me you don't love me," Jonah demanded. "Tell me you don't feel the same as I do."

"It doesn't matter what I feel," she said with tears streaming down her cheeks. "Nothing can come from our feelings."

"Why?"

"Because—"

Just then, there was a loud crash from Charles's room. Jonah raced out the door and Mariah was left alone.

She'd almost told him. She'd almost explained the reason she could never marry him. The reason the two of them didn't have a future together.

That was the only way she could convince him that it didn't matter what they meant to each other, what he thought their kisses meant. Nothing meant anything. He could not marry her.

She could not give him what he needed.

CHAPTER SEVEN

J ONAH HADN'T BEEN able to leave Charles's side for nearly two days. The opium in his body refused to let go of him. Every time Jonah thought the drug was finally out of his friend's body, it grabbed hold of him and clung on with a ferociousness that said his battle was not yet over.

If Mariah had come to see Charles, it must have been during one of the brief times that Jonah was able to close his eyes. If she'd come at all, he hadn't seen her.

Finally, on the seventh day, Charles opened his eyes and seemed to recognize his surroundings.

"Hello," Jonah said. He leaned over Charles and held a glass of water to his lips.

The patient took several huge gulps of the water, then collapsed back against his pillow.

"Is it finally over?"

"Nearly. Just a few more days. But the worst is over."

"Is Mari here?"

"Yes. She just stepped out for a moment."

Jonah couldn't tell Charles that he hadn't seen Mariah for several days—that she'd avoided him since the last time they kissed.

"How long will I be here?"

"For several more weeks," Jonah answered. "You don't want

to leave until you've completely removed any part of the poison that was in your body."

"Then I won't crave it anymore?"

"I wish that were the case. You will want the opium you relied on for the rest of your life. But each day you will want it less than you did the day before, until finally the day will arrive when you won't think of it at all."

"I can't wait for that day."

"It will be a day to celebrate."

"Can you tell Mari that I'd like to see her?"

"Of course, Charles. I'll be right back."

Jonah left to find Mariah. He first went to her rooms, which were empty. As he turned to leave, laughter from beyond the glass-paneled door drew him to the garden, where he found her.

She sat on a bench that overlooked a bed of burgundy begonias. He smiled. It wasn't laughter he'd heard. Mariah had been singing.

He stepped up to her, so quietly that she didn't hear him at first. When she did, she turned her head. Her eyes opened wide and her breath caught.

"Your brother is awake."

"Oh," she said with excitement in her voice.

"He wants to see you."

"Oh," she repeated, then rose to her feet.

She took her first step away from him, but he stopped her. "Mariah, please," he said, stepping in front of her. "We can't go on like this. We need to talk."

"Not now, Jonah."

"Then when?"

"Not now," she insisted, then stepped around him and sped away.

Jonah sat on the bench where he'd found her and tried to think. Something was wrong. She was hiding something from him. She cared for him. Her kisses told him she did. Yet she was adamant in her denial. She refused to admit how she felt. Why?

He rose from the bench and paced a few feet along the path. He couldn't rest until he forced her to give him the reason for her refusal to admit that she cared for him. He wasn't sure he could survive without her. Wasn't sure he could live his life if she wasn't a part of it. She was too important to him. She possessed too much of his heart.

More frustrated than ever, Jonah returned to Charles's room and opened the door. Mariah knelt by the bed and held her brother's hand. They were talking quietly, and she was smiling at him while she wiped his face with a damp cloth and combed his hair. Her eyes were filled with tears, but this time they were tears of joy.

"Charlie is better," she said, turning to look at Jonah.

"Yes, he's much better."

"Thank you, Jonah," she whispered.

"You're welcome, Mariah. It will be good to have your brother back."

She nodded and smiled at him.

"Why don't you go to the kitchen and ask Cook for two butter sandwiches and some hot tea?" he said. "Charles should be hungry after going without anything to eat for so long."

"Yes," she answered.

Jonah held out his hand and helped Mariah to her feet. He was silent when he opened the door and closed it when she left.

"You've made your sister very happy," Jonah said to Charles.

"Yes, but from the look on her face, you haven't made *her* very happy," Charles said with a serious expression.

Jonah sat down in the chair beside the bed. "No, I haven't. I kissed her."

"She didn't like it?"

"She liked it quite a great deal, if I'm any judge." He swept a hand through his hair. "And so did I."

"So, what's wrong?"

"I told Mariah I cared for her. Actually, I told her I more than cared for her."

"And?"

"She told me I couldn't. That she didn't have anything to give me."

"I see," Charles said.

"What happened to her, Charles?"

"I don't know."

"Oh come now, man, you have to. Something had to have happened to her. Something that has affected her deeply. Made her afraid to marry."

Charles's face paled and his eyes lowered.

"What?" Jonah asked. "What was it? Was she in the same accident as you?"

Charles slowly lifted his head. "Yes."

"What happened to her?"

"I don't know. No one would ever talk about it, but I know it was serious. The doctor told Mother that she'd lost so much blood she would probably die. And even if she did live, she would probably never be the same."

"What did he mean by that?"

"I don't know. No one has ever spoken more of it. Ever. But I know it was serious."

At that moment the door opened, and Mariah entered the room. "Cook even sent up a small bowl of broth. She said you were such a fine, strapping young man that you needed to build your strength."

Jonah couldn't help but smile. "Cook has taken a shine to you, Charles. She takes a shine to all the handsome young men, which means you can expect special treatment from now on."

"What does that mean?" Charles said with a smile.

"Extra desserts, and larger portions of your favorite foods for starters."

"Are you jealous, Jonah?" Charles asked, taking a bite of the sandwich Mariah held out to him.

"Oh, no," Jonah answered. "You may be toward the top of her list of favorites, but I'm number one and always will be."

Mariah laughed at the banter between her brother and Jonah. She seemed to be relaxing as she held the glass of ale to Charles's mouth and he took a healthy swallow.

"When he's finished, make him go to sleep, Mariah," Jonah said. "He needs to rest. He may feel on top of the world now, but that will soon fade. His body has gone through a great deal and will need time to adapt to all the changes he's experienced."

She nodded. Her expression held more relief than it had earlier, but she was still somewhat guarded when she looked at Jonah.

She was holding something back from him. Something that was the cause of the stress between them. And Jonah refused to give up until he knew what that was.

IT HAD BEEN one week since Charles had gone through the worst of his treatment. One week since Jonah had last been with Mariah. One week since he'd last kissed her. And she avoided him as if he had the plague. He didn't know what to do to break through the wall she'd erected to protect herself from him.

One thing he really wanted to do was to take Charles and Mariah to meet Jack and Annie. Hopefully, Annie could talk to Charles and tell him her experience being dependent on opium. But most of all, maybe Mariah would find someone she could talk to. Jonah prayed she would.

He had a steward bring his carriage to the front before he went to Mariah's sitting room. Charles was no doubt there with her. Jonah knocked on the door.

"Yes?" he heard Mariah say.

Jonah opened the door and stepped inside the room. "Oh, good," he said. "I was hoping I'd find you both here. How would you like to take a short ride?"

"Sounds ideal," Charles said, rising to his feet.

"Where are we going?" she asked.

"I'd like you to meet some friends of mine, Major Jack Washburn and his wife, Annie. Hope's House is located on Burnhaven, their estate."

"Really?" Charles said. "Then I'll be glad to meet them. And thank them."

"Jack and Annie will be glad to meet you, too. They enjoy meeting every patient who comes here for help."

Jonah held out his arm, and Mariah placed her fingers on his sleeve. He ignored his body's reaction when she touched him and led her to the carriage. Charles followed.

When they reached the mansion, Jonah stepped out of the carriage and helped Mariah to the ground. The press of her fingers against the palm of his hand caused lightning bolts to travel down his spine. The jerk of her hand from his told Jonah she experienced a similar reaction. He wanted to shift his gaze to meet hers so she knew he had the same feeling, but knew not to.

"Dr. Reynolds," Jewel, the butler, greeted Jonah at the door.

"Good afternoon, Jewel. Are the major and Lady Anne available?"

"Yes, I'll show you up. They'll be glad to see you. They thought you were still gone."

"No, I returned several weeks ago."

"I won't tell them that," the butler said with a smile. "They'll be disappointed that you haven't called on them before now."

"Yes, but I've been busy."

"Of course, Dr. Reynolds."

Jewel led them up the stairs and knocked on a receiving room door. "You have guests, Major. My lady."

Jewel stepped back, and Jonah escorted Mariah and Charles into the room.

"Jonah!" Annie called out. She ran across the room and wrapped her arms around Jonah in an eager hug.

"Jonah," Jack said, grasping Jonah's hand. "What a surprise. We didn't know you were back."

"I brought some friends to meet you," Jonah said, bringing

Mariah and Charles forward. "Jack, Annie, this is Lady Mariah and her brother Charles, the Earl of Aspen."

"My lord," Jack and Annie greeted him. "Lady Mariah."

"Have you come as patients?" Annie asked.

"I am the patient," Charles answered, casting his eyes down slightly.

"Oh. I hope I haven't embarrassed you."

"Not at all, my lady," he replied.

"It's only that Jonah is so wonderful," Annie said. "I'm always in awe when I meet another patient he has cured."

Mariah turned her gaze to Jack. "Were you a patient?" she asked him.

"No, my husband wasn't Jonah's patient," Annie said. "I was."

"Oh!" Mariah said. "I'm sorry. I shouldn't have asked."

She turned her attention to Jonah, and he smiled at her. "That's all right, Mariah. Annie is eager to talk about her experience. She's proud of the progress she made, as she should be."

"I was one of Jonah's first patients," Annie said. "He saved my marriage and gave me back my life."

"I see," Mariah said as her gaze locked with Jonah's.

A warmth settled around his heart again, as it did every time Mariah looked at him.

"It was a long time ago, but I am still indebted to him," Annie added. "I don't know what Jack or I would have done without him."

"You're going to give me a big head if you continue with your compliments, Annie," Jonah said, holding up his hands.

"You deserve every compliment you get, Jonah. The good you do for anyone with a dependence on opium cannot be stated enough. I sing your praises whenever I have the opportunity."

"I know. That is why I am at risk of getting that big head I'm concerned about."

"You are too modest a man to get a big head, Jonah."

"Thank you for the compliment, Annie, but why don't you

take Mariah to the nursery and introduce her to your children?"

"I'd love to," Annie said. "We just had our third child two months ago," she said, getting to her feet. She walked to the door. "If we're fortunate, they will all be asleep. That way you can think they are the angels I tell everyone they are."

>>>><<<<

MARIAH LAUGHED AS she and Annie entered the nursery. As hoped, the three babes were still asleep.

"Oh, Annie. They are adorable."

"This is Julia, our eldest. She happens to be too smart for her own good." Annie stepped to the second bed. "This is Frank. He was named after Jack's father. And this," she said, stepping to the small baby in a crib, "is Jonah. I'm sure you can imagine who he was named after."

A broad smile lifted the corners of Mariah's mouth. "Yes. I can guess."

"You love children, don't you?" Annie said, hooking her arm through Mariah's and pulling her close. "Someday soon I know you will have your own."

Mariah summoned a smile. "I'm not sure that will ever happen."

"Of course it will. Anyone with two eyes in their head can see that you and Jonah are head over ears in love with each other."

Mariah tried to pretend that Annie's words didn't rip her heart from her breast, but before she could stop it from happening, the smile left her face and her eyes filled with tears.

CHAPTER EIGHT

"OH, MARIAH," ANNIE said, wrapping her arms around Mariah and holding her tight.

"I'm sorry," Mariah said. "I'm usually much better at controlling my emotions."

"There's nothing to apologize for. You need someone to talk to, and I'm just the person to listen to you. Here," Annie said, and led her from the nursery to a private sitting room where they wouldn't be disturbed. "Sit down," she said, then called for a tea tray and a bottle of brandy.

"Now," Annie said when the tea and brandy arrived. "Take this," she said, handing Mariah a cup of tea with a dash of brandy in it.

Mariah took a sip of her tea and let the warm liquor go down her throat.

"Now, tell me what is wrong."

Mariah lifted her chin and smiled a weak smile. A part of her wanted to bare her soul to Annie and tell her the entire story. A part of her wanted to tell her that, more than anything, she wanted to have a family with Jonah. But she couldn't. A part of her wanted to admit how much she loved him and didn't think she could ever get along without him. But she did not dare. No one could know how lacking she would be as a wife and mother.

"It's nothing, Annie. It's just been a very stressful time for me, with Charles going through treatments, and my sister on the verge of getting engaged, and my mother having to handle all the details while I'm here with my brother. I'm just letting everything bother me."

"Are you sure it doesn't have anything to do with Jonah?"

"Jonah?" Mariah asked, pretending ignorance.

"Yes," Annie answered. "You love him. Anyone with eyes half open can see that you do. I could tell you did the first time you looked at him."

"You must be mistaken, Annie. I don't love him. I like him. I always have. I've known him forever. He's like a brother to me."

"Are you sure that's all you feel for him?"

"Of course."

"What about Jonah? How does he feel about you?"

Mariah struggled to appear surprised by the question. "How does he feel about me?" She chuckled. "I doubt he even thinks about me."

Annie's eyebrows lifted. "Where did you first see Jonah when he returned to London?"

"At a ball. I can't tell you how surprised I was to see that he'd returned to London."

"Why do you think he returned?"

"He told me his brother wrote him and asked him to return."

Annie looked puzzled. "I didn't even know Jonah had a brother."

"Yes. An older brother. He's the Earl of Aspen."

"Jonah is the son of an earl?"

"Yes. The second son. When Jonah's father found out Jonah wanted to become a doctor, he said he wouldn't allow it. No son of his would take up such a lowly occupation. Jonah was forced to leave, and he never returned until now."

"Is his father still alive?"

"No. I think that's why Jonah's brother asked him to come back, to repair the damage their father did by sending him away." Mariah forced a smile. "I also think he wanted to show Jonah around London and introduce him to all the eligible young ladies in an attempt for him to find the perfect female to marry. That's essential, you know."

"Why?" Annie asked.

"Jonah's brother has four children, all girls. And the doctor warned them that his wife's heart would not survive another pregnancy. Therefore, it's Jonah's responsibility to produce an heir, plus possibly a spare."

Annie's face brightened. "I'm afraid I don't see the problem, Mariah. This is perfect. Jonah's the son of nobility, and you are the daughter of nobility. He wants children, and it's obvious that you love children. You are both madly in love with each other. This arrangement couldn't be more perfect."

"I wish that were true," Mariah whispered.

"What did you say?" Annie asked just as the baby let out a loud cry. "Excuse me," she said as she rose. "If I don't pick him up, he'll cry until he wakes the other children." She went into the next room and came back carrying baby Jonah in her arms. "Would you like to hold him?"

"I'd love to," Mariah said, then took the baby from Annie.

The baby wasn't satisfied being held on Mariah's lap, so she stood with him, put him over her shoulder, and paced the room.

"You have a way with children," Annie said when baby Jonah immediately quieted.

"I've had experience," Mariah said. "My younger sister, Felicity, was born when I was old enough to help take care of her. Mama had a difficult birth and needed a great deal of bed rest after, so much of Felicity's care was left to me."

"It is evident. You are a natural caregiver."

"I enjoy taking care of people."

"Speaking of taking care of people," Annie said, "would you mind if I slip down to check on the men? I just need to see if they require anything."

"No," Mariah said. "You go ahead. Little Jonah is almost asleep. I'll be down as soon as he falls asleep."

"You're a doll, Mariah. Are you sure you'll be all right up here by yourself?"

"Of course. I'll enjoy the peace and quiet."

Annie walked to the door and left Mariah to herself. She rocked the baby in her arms until he fell asleep, then sat with him in the rocking chair. He slept for quite a while, and Mariah took the opportunity to consider what she'd told Annie.

She hadn't said anything she'd vowed not to tell anyone, but that didn't make her feel better. She'd really wanted to share what was truly bothering her. She'd wanted to rip open the burden she carried, but knew she couldn't tell Annie the secret she was keeping from Jonah before she'd told him. It wouldn't be fair for anyone else to know why she could never marry before it was revealed to him.

She placed the baby in his cradle, then took a cloth and cooled her face. If she avoided looking at Jonah, hopefully he would never know she'd been crying. Even if he did, she could make up an excuse to deny the redness in her eyes.

Mariah went down the stairs and walked into the room where the men sat. She tried to avoid looking at him and thought she managed well, but even though she tried, she knew Jonah was aware that she was troubled. She walked past him and sat down where he couldn't look directly at her.

Thankfully, Jack and Charles kept the conversation going, and she wasn't the object of his attention.

SOMETHING WAS WRONG. When Mariah and Annie returned from the nursery, Jonah could tell as soon as he looked in her eyes that Mariah had been crying. Oh, there was a smile on her face, the same as Annie had on hers, but neither of their smiles reached their eyes. Neither of their smiles seemed sincere.

"You have a beautiful family, Major Washburn," Mariah said.

"If you are a friend of Jonah's, then you must call me Jack."

"Very well," she said with a faux smile. "You have a beautiful family, Jack."

"Thank you, but all the credit goes to my wife. She passed down her beauty as well as her intelligence to each one of our children."

Jonah watched as Annie reached out and twined Jack's fingers in hers. The look they exchanged spoke of a love that was still as fierce as it had been the day he met them. Jonah knew Mariah felt the same about him. He just couldn't understand why she refused to acknowledge that what they felt for each other was the same kind of lasting love that Jack and Annie shared.

"While you two ladies were in the nursery admiring our storybook children, Jonah, Lord Aspen, and I were down here making plans," Jack said with a teasing glint in his eyes.

"That sounds interesting," Annie said. "Pray tell, what plans have the three of you concocted?"

"Jonah said he has a new patient arriving at Hope's House in a few days, so he couldn't plan anything until the middle of next week, but then he, Lord Aspen, and Lady Mariah will return. They will spend the night, and in the morning, we will rise early and travel to visit Livie and Theo."

"That's a wonderful idea, darling," she said with boundless enthusiasm. "Then you can meet our good friends, Theo and Livie Dunworthy. They run the Angel's Wings Orphanage and Foundling home. They're a remarkable couple. I know you'll love them the minute you meet them."

Jack shifted his gaze between Mariah and her brother. "Jonah knows Theo and Livie. He'll have to tell you all about them and what they do."

"Yes," Annie added. "They also own a shop in London, the Angel's Wings Jams and Jellies."

"Jams and jellies?" Charles said incredulously. "That is quite a wide range of occupations, isn't it?"

"The jam and jelly shop is what provides an income for the

orphanage. It's become quite a moneymaking project," Jack added.

"Remarkable," Charles said. Everyone could tell he was duly impressed.

"We decided we could spend the day with Theo and Livie, then return here before dark. Mariah, Jonah, and Lord Aspen can spend the night, then travel on to Hope's House in the morning."

"That's a wonderful idea," Annie said enthusiastically.

"What do you think, Mariah?" Jonah asked when he saw a hint of hesitation in Mariah's eyes.

"I'd love to meet your friends," she replied. "They sound like an interesting couple."

"They are," Jonah said, keeping his gaze locked with hers. He couldn't help but feel that there was something that bothered her. He still couldn't tell what it was, but he wasn't about to give up until he knew.

"I'd love to stretch my legs a bit before we sit for lunch," he said, getting to his feet. "Mariah, would you like to take a walk through Annie's garden? Please," he added when she didn't answer immediately.

"Of course," she said, then rose when he extended his hand to escort her to the terrace.

"Would you care for me to accompany you?" Charles asked.

"No," Jonah answered firmly. "Why don't you remain behind and chat with Annie? She suffered the same affliction that you did."

Charles turned to Annie, and she engaged him in conversation while Jonah escorted Mariah to the garden.

"What is wrong, Mariah?" he asked when they reached the path in the garden. "And don't tell me nothing, because it's obvious that something is. You've been crying."

"Yes, I have," Mariah admitted.

"What were you crying about?"

He looped her hand through his elbow and led her farther down the garden path. When they reached the first bench along the way, he led her to it and sat down beside her.

"We need to talk," he said, gathering her hands in his.

"Yes, we do, but I'd prefer not to talk here."

"Where would you like to talk?"

"At Hope's House. When we return."

"Is there a reason you want to wait?"

"I'm enjoying my time here. And I think you are, too. I don't want to spoil it."

"And you think that what you have to tell me will upset me?"

"And me too. It will upset both of us."

He saw the pain in her eyes. "What can I do, Mariah?"

"There's nothing, Jonah," she said, then lifted her hand and cupped his cheek in her palm. "There is nothing either of us can do. I wish there were. But there is not."

He covered her hand and kept it anchored there. Then he lowered his head and pressed his mouth to hers.

He was afraid she would turn her head and break off their kiss, but she didn't. In fact, she accepted his kiss with a desperation that surprised him.

She opened her mouth and allowed him to skim the roof of her mouth, then brush against her teeth. Her tongue battled with his, fighting for dominance. Even though she'd never been the aggressor, she was today. It was as if she couldn't get enough of his kisses.

Jonah deepened his kiss, demanded as much as she offered him. No matter how much he gave her, she seemed to want more.

He kissed her again and again, until their breaths came in ragged gasps. "I love you, Mariah," he said in a harsh whisper.

"I love you too, Jonah," she gasped. "But that doesn't matter. No matter how much we think we love each other, it doesn't matter. I can't give you what you want."

"What is it that you think I want that you cannot give me?"

Mariah cupped his face again and lifted her head until her mouth met his. Her kiss was brief, but it was passionate.

"Answer me, Mariah. What is it you don't think you can give me?"

"The one thing you need."

"What, Mariah? What can't you give me?"

"Children, Jonah. I can't give you children. I'm barren."

Tears filled Mariah's eyes, and she rose to her feet and walked away from him.

Jonah called her back, but she continued toward the house.

CHAPTER NINE

T HEY RETURNED TO Hope's House later that day. Mariah had hardly spoken all the way home. She couldn't. It hurt too much to explain what she'd said.

She tried to recall Jonah's reaction. He hadn't said anything at all, except call to her to return to him.

He didn't understand. He'd heard her words stating that she was barren, but it was as if he hadn't been able to comprehend them, or understand how they affected him.

But they did. More than he knew.

She knew that it was only a matter of time before she would have to have a conversation with Jonah. Only a matter of time until he forced her to spell out in unmistakable words exactly what she'd meant. And she dreaded the arrival of that day. She was a coward, and avoided being with Jonah as much as she could.

She was given a reprieve, however, because the next day Charles had a difficult day, and she was forced to spend most of her time with him. He was so much better, but in random moments his nerves seemed on edge. She tried to keep him occupied when he had one of those days.

Before they'd left Burnhaven, Jonah and Charles made plans with Jack and Annie that they would all meet again in a week. They would spend the night at Burnhaven, then travel to the

Angel's Wings Orphanage and Foundling Home. Since it was only a little more than an hour's trip by carriage, they would have most of the day to spend with Theo and Livie.

Mariah wasn't looking forward to the trip. She was, however, looking forward to meeting Theo and Livie. Jonah had told her and Charles all about them and the work they did to find homes for the orphaned children. They also provided for them and made sure they were happy and well cared for. Because of Livie and Theo's love for each other, their dedication to the children made for a very happy environment.

Mariah knew that if Theo was anything like Jack, he was a remarkable man. He'd been a soldier, just like Jack, and had devoted his life to serving his country. She did look forward to meeting him and Livie.

What she wasn't looking forward to was spending time with the orphans. Meeting with babies she would never have. Watching the toddlers learn to walk and try to talk and play with each other. Holding children that desperately needed the mother she would never be. Pretending that her heart wasn't being torn in two because she would never have her own babes to nestle in her arms. Pretending that she could ignore the gaping hole in her chest where a child's sweet smile should live. And she could never give Jonah the children he so desperately wanted and needed.

Seeing the babes that Annie and Livie had given their husbands would make it all worse. According to Charles, there was a third soldier who was a friend of Jack and Theo's. Quinn and his wife were raising Quinn's brother's two young daughters and had a set of triplet boys of their own. They had also just had a third daughter. How was it possible for everyone to be so blessed—except Mariah?

She chastised herself. Self-pity was something she'd never allowed herself to wallow in. She had no one to blame for what had happened to her but herself. Charles had warned her not to take such a chance when they raced. He'd told her not to jump that hedge, but she'd refused to listen to him. She had always been stubborn, and she was paying for it.

Mariah mulled over all these problems with no relief. All she had were endless questions with no answers. All she had were worrisome thoughts with no solutions.

Finally, she rose from her bed and walked out into the garden. She couldn't sleep and needed a change of scenery. She needed to take her mind off the things that caused her to feel sorry for herself—a malady she'd suffered from since they'd returned from Jack and Annie's two days prior.

Jonah had only one day to rest up before his new patient arrived. Mariah had met the new fellow at dinner the night before. Ralph Watson had charmed them all in a comfortable way. He seemed extraordinarily nice—a handsome man with a pleasing smile and eyes that sparkled when he spoke.

He was a boxer by trade and was considered by many to be one of the best in London. She could easily see why. His shoulders were nearly as wide as a doorframe, and his arms displayed more muscular brawn than most men's. He stood well over six feet and had long, dark hair that curled at the ends.

All through dinner he'd talked mostly about his wife and the three children she'd given him. He loved being a father, and because of his success in the boxing ring, he'd provided for his wife and family, with money left over. Until the day he was convinced that he could improve his boxing by taking opium.

But opium didn't make him a better boxer. It changed him from the man he'd been into a wild person who wasn't in control of his actions. A violent man who didn't realize when he'd gone too far. Until the night he nearly killed his opponent.

Now, boxers in the circuit were afraid of him. They refused to get in the ring with him.

Suddenly, he could no longer earn a living from boxing. He could no longer earn enough to put food on the table for his children.

His wife still loved him, but opium had ruined his marriage.

She refused to stay with him and starve, so she took their three children and went to live with her parents. She told him she wouldn't return until he no longer used opium. Which was why he'd come to Jonah for help. He was desperate to be the boxer he'd been before he started taking opium.

Mariah talked to him for several minutes, then wished him luck and told him she was proud of him for cleansing himself from the poison that was destroying his body. She was moved by the way his eyes watered a bit when she said she could say for certain that his wife would be so very proud of him. When he finished his meal, he left the table and went to his room to begin his treatment.

Mariah stepped across a small bridge as she continued to ruminate on the men's conversation the previous night. How they'd been understanding, encouraging to the fellow, and not at all judgmental. It pleased her immensely, though it did not at all surprise her.

A small shudder made her realize she'd stood on the little bridge a bit too long. The chill breeze sent her back inside. Not ready to return to her bed, Mariah went to the library and searched through the books on the shelves for something to read.

Finally, she found something that sounded interesting. A book by Jane Austen. She'd read *Pride and Prejudice* and had truly enjoyed it. This was titled *Sense and Sensibility*. She was sure she'd enjoy this book, as well.

Locating a cushioned chair in a corner of the library, she made herself comfortable and opened the book. Before she'd finished reading the first page, she heard a loud bellow from the top of the stairs leading to the male patients' rooms. Then another roar and several footsteps racing up the stairs.

Mariah was sure she wouldn't have heard the loud roars if the library wasn't directly below the room where the noise had come from, but she was close enough that she couldn't help but hear it.

There was more noise, followed by loud grunts and groans, then the sound of more footsteps.

Mariah knew the sounds were coming from Ralph Watson's room. The boxer was having a difficult time fighting off the opium terrors that had a hold of his body. From the sounds coming from his room, every assistant in Hope's House must be there assisting Jonah.

Curiosity got the better of her, and she rose from her chair and opened the library door. As she looked out, another assistant raced up the stairs carrying several lengths of thick, heavy rope. She wasn't sure what they intended to do with that, unless Jonah had opted to confine Ralph to his bed.

For the first time, she realized how dangerous Jonah's work could be. And she was reminded again how controlling opium was. This man was a professional boxer. The opium in him had indeed unleashed a monster.

Mariah listened for several more minutes, but the sounds continued. Ralph was fighting the ropes. Little by little, however, he seemed to submit to their control. The struggling didn't cease, but it didn't seem as intense as it had been before.

She listened a while longer until Ralph's door opened and Jonah stepped into the hall.

Blood ran down his face from a cut above his right eye and another cut down his left cheek. He staggered to the top of the stairs and braced his outstretched arms against the railing.

A knot clenched in Mariah's stomach, and she raced up to Jonah to help him down the stairs. His shirt was covered in blood and his face was beginning to turn black and blue.

"Hold on to me," she said, wrapping her arm around his waist. "Put your arm around my shoulders."

He did, and she led him to her sitting room.

"Remind me never to get in the ring with Ralph Watson," he said on a gasp.

"Sit down."

She led him to the settee and helped him sit. When she was certain he wasn't going to faint, she reached for a basin of water and several cloths and began washing his face.

"Some of these cuts might need to be stitched," she said.

"I think it's already too late to stitch them. They're too swollen."

Mariah rinsed the cloths and dabbed at his face again. When she had him mostly cleaned, she took the basin away and returned with fresh water. "Lie down," she said, and helped him lie back against the cushions. When he was prone, she removed his shoes. "Is your face the only place you're hurt?" she asked.

"I don't know," he answered. "I hurt all over."

His shirt was so bloodstained that she removed it and checked his chest. There was a long cut where he'd been scratched, and another long scratch on his back.

"What did he scratch you with?" she asked after she pulled the formerly white shirt over his head.

"I'm not sure," he said, groaning. "I think it must have been his fingernails."

"He definitely defeated you, didn't he?" she said in a teasing tone.

"Yes. He is one of the most violent patients I've ever treated."

"No wonder no one wanted to get in the ring with him," she said. "He told me that he turned violent when he was under the influence."

"I've never seen anyone in such a rage. Most people aren't *that* violent."

Mariah went to the medicine chest to retrieve a small jar of salve. She applied it to all the places where his skin was broken. "I'm sorry," she said when he sucked in a harsh breath. "I'm trying to be gentle."

"I know you are. I guess I just make a better doctor than a patient."

"That's what they say. Doctors make the worst patients."

Once she had covered the scratches and gashes with bandages, Mariah reached for a cover and placed it over Jonah.

"Thank you, Mariah."

"Of course."

He reached for her hand and held it. "When are we going to talk?"

"I don't know, Jonah. There's just so much work for you, I don't see when we'll have time."

Mariah pulled her hand from his and rose. She went to the cupboard and took out a decanter of whiskey.

"Here, drink this," she said, pouring some of the liquor into a glass.

Jonah seemed grateful to accept it.

"That should help," she said.

"Yes," he muttered, then closed his eyes and fell asleep.

She needed to talk to him soon. She knew that. But in light of recent events, it would have to wait until morning.

MARIAH REMINDED HERSELF that today was the day she would speak to Jonah, but she always came up with a reason to put their conversation off for another hour, another day. Then she thought it might be better to wait until they went to meet Theo and Livie. She didn't want to ruin what promised to be a pleasant outing.

It had been a week since Jonah battled Ralph Watson. His bruises and cuts were much better, but the fact that he'd been in a fight was still evident. However, he'd decided they couldn't put off their trip to Theo and Livie's, so Mariah was packing an extra gown to wear tomorrow, then waiting for Charles to tell her it was time to go.

"Are you almost ready to leave?" her brother asked from the doorway.

"Yes, are you?"

"I'm very ready," he answered. "I don't know why, but I'm actually looking forward to spending a few days away from Hope's House. I think that means I'm almost ready to return to London and get my life back."

"What does Jonah say?"

"Yesterday he said it usually takes about a month before most people feel confident enough to be out on their own."

"Well," Mariah said, putting on her bonnet and locating her reticule and parasol, "it will be a month at the end of the week." She stepped to where her brother stood and grabbed his hands. "I can't tell you how proud I am of you, Charles. I know how difficult this was for you, but you mastered it with flying colors."

"Thank you, Mari. I couldn't have done it without you."

"Yes, you could have, Charles. You're much stronger than you think you are. It's just that you have relied on the opium so long that you forgot how strong a person you actually are."

Charles gave her hand a gentle squeeze, then took the bag she'd packed and escorted her from the room.

"Are you ready to go?" Jonah said as he came up behind them.

"Yes," Mariah said. "I'm looking forward to meeting your friends."

They walked outside, and Jonah lowered the step to help her into the carriage.

"How are you feeling?" she asked him when he entered the carriage and sat in the seat opposite her.

"Each day I feel a little less *bruised*."

"How is Mr. Watson doing?"

"He's still working his way out of the opium's grasp, but he's improving."

The carriage jerked into motion, and Mariah saw Jonah wince when the movement jolted him. "Did you bring anything to help with the pain?" she asked.

Jonah smiled. "Why, Mariah, I'm surprised. I didn't think you would encourage me to drink so early in the day."

She smiled back at him. "I'm not, Dr. Reynolds. I only thought a little whiskey might help you tolerate the ride with minimal groaning."

"How thoughtful of you," he said, then bent over and pulled

a small basket from under the seat. "As it so happens," he said, "I have just such a bottle hidden here."

Mariah reached out and took the bottle from his hand, then she leaned over and took a glass out of the basket and poured some whiskey into the glass. "Drink this," she said when she handed the glass back to him.

"This is hardly enough to wet my tongue," he complained.

"It will just have to do," Mariah replied with a wink.

Jonah took a sip from the glass, then breathed a heavy sigh.

"Does it help?" she asked.

"Yes," he said, and took another sip. "I could swear Watson cracked a rib or two. Or ten."

"He is definitely a strong man."

"That he is. It's a good thing not many of our patients are as strong as he is. I'd have to hire bodyguards to handle them."

Mariah smiled.

Jonah looked over and checked on Charles. His head was propped against the corner of the carriage, and he was snoring softly. "Why do I think that even though you tell me you're anxious to meet Livie and Theo, you really aren't that excited?"

"Perhaps you're imagining it," she said, clutching her hands in her lap.

He shook his head. "No, I don't think so. The smile on your face definitely died when you found out they manage an orphanage."

Mariah focused on the scenery beyond the carriage window. Jonah was far too observant. He knew her too well and understood so much about her.

"Are we nearly there?" she asked, hoping to divert the conversation.

"Yes, we're almost there. Why are you so desperate to change the subject?"

"I'm not. I just don't have an answer for something you are imagining."

"Sometimes you are quite frustrating, do you know that?" he

asked with a glimmer in his eyes.

"Yes," she answered. "What was Annie's story? How did she get drawn into the opium world?"

"It was a sad story," he said, sighing. "Her stepbrother forced her to take laudanum until she was dependent upon it."

"Why?"

"He was jealous of Jack. He was in love with Annie and wanted her for himself. He thought if he made her undesirable in Jack's eyes, Jack would reject her and she'd turn to him. But Jack loved her too much to leave her. Their love was too strong."

"Oh, how beautiful. I knew there was something magical about those two."

"The same as there's something magical in the love I feel for you," Jonah added.

Mariah's heart stuttered in her breast, and she lowered her head. "Don't, Jonah."

"Why, Mariah? Why do you refuse to admit that you love me?"

"Because I can't. It can't be. I told you that."

She was prepared to reaffirm the reason she'd given him previously when the carriage turned down a broad lane and stopped in front of Jack and Annie's country home. A footman hurried to open the carriage door and lower the steps. Jonah stepped out first and helped Mariah from the carriage. Charles followed.

"Welcome," Jack and Annie greeted them as they rushed forward to meet them. "We've been waiting for you to arrive," Annie said, giving Mariah a welcoming hug.

"I received word from Theo. He and Livie can't wait to meet you," Jack said, clapping Jonah and Charles on the backs.

"I can't wait to meet them either," Charles said. "Or to taste some of the jam and jelly they make."

"We always have a supply of the jellies and jams on hand. I'll make sure Cook serves samples of each with afternoon tea and breakfast in the morning."

"I'm already looking forward to both meals."

"I imagine you're starving. I'll have Cook serve lunch immediately."

"Ever since I gave up opium, I'm hungry all the time," Charles said.

"I was the same way," Annie chimed in. "I'm glad that lessens pretty quickly, or I wouldn't fit through any of our doorways."

"You're perfect any way you are," Jack said, wrapping his arm around her shoulders. "I wouldn't want you any other way."

Annie stood on her tiptoes and kissed him on the lips.

"Let me show you to your rooms," she said when she broke the kiss. "I'll give you a little time to get refreshed, then we'll eat lunch. I imagine you rose early to arrive already, so you're no doubt in need of a nap once we finish lunch."

"That sounds ideal," Jonah said on a laugh.

"That's because Jonah hasn't managed much sleep lately," Mariah said. "He'll have to tell you about his latest patient. A professional boxer, and he used Jonah as a punching bag."

"Oh no," Annie said. "Are you all right?"

"Yes," Jonah answered. "But I'm glad we're out of that carriage. I don't remember there being so many ruts in the road the last time we were here."

"He just needs to rest a little while," Mariah said.

"Yes, doctor," he teased, and everyone laughed.

Annie led them up to their rooms and told them Cook would ring the dinner bell when lunch was ready. They all retired for a little while, and Mariah lay on the bed and tried to close her eyes, but sleep wouldn't come.

She knew time was running short and she was going to be forced to explain what she'd said to Jonah the other night. She knew he didn't believe her. Not really. Many women believed they couldn't conceive for various reasons, and falsely assumed they were barren when they weren't. But she *was* barren, and when Jonah discovered the truth of it, he'd be forced to face the fact that they could never marry.

There was no way around it, and it would be better to talk to him when they were surrounded by his friends. Besides, it would be impossible for her to be surrounded by the babies and infants in the orphanage and hide her feelings for the children she wanted yet would never have.

No matter how hard she tried to hide the fact that she yearned for children but was unable to have any, Jonah would see right through her and know there was something wrong.

She wouldn't be able to hide her secret from him any longer, so she might as well force him to face the truth right now.

CHAPTER TEN

M ARIAH STROLLED ONTO the terrace after dinner that night
and waited. She knew Jonah would notice she hadn't gone
to bed and would come after her. He always seemed to know
where she was and checked to make sure she was all right. She
loved him for that.

But she wasn't all right.

She wrapped her arms around her waist and took in a deep
breath, then slowly released it when she heard his footsteps cross
the terrace toward her. A warm, comforting wave washed
through her as her whole body acknowledged his presence. She
stiffened, hoping she could banish it and knowing at the same
time that she couldn't.

"I thought you'd have gone to bed by now," he said as he
eased himself into a chair next to her.

"I was waiting for you."

Jonah laughed. "You knew I would come, did you?"

"Yes. At least, I hoped you would."

He slid his chair around the table so he could look directly at
her. "It sounds as if you have something important to speak with
me about."

"I do, Jonah."

"It also sounds as if I'm not going to like what you have to
say."

"Probably not. But it has to be said."

"Does this have anything to do with what you said the other night when you walked away from me?"

"Yes," she answered in a whisper.

Jonah reached for her hand. "Then perhaps it's best that you say what's on your mind and we get what's bothering you out into the open."

"Yes, it's best to get this out into the open."

"Very well, Mariah. Please, begin."

"First, let me say that I have always been in love with you, Jonah. From the time you and Charles became friends. I remember following you around like a lovesick puppy."

A smile lit Jonah's face.

"Charles used to get so angry with me. He threatened to lock me in my room when you came over so I couldn't follow you. But I told him it wouldn't help. I'd scream and pound on the door until one of the maids heard me and let me out. Then he'd get in trouble for locking me in my room and be the one who had to go without supper."

"You were quite the devious one, weren't you?"

"Yes, I was. But I was in love."

Jonah picked up her hand and twined his fingers in hers. "You were far wiser than I was. I didn't realize that I loved you until I left home, and Father told me I could never return. You were the only person I missed."

"I missed you, too. I turned a little wild. If my parents told me I couldn't do something, I made a point of doing exactly what they wouldn't allow me to do. Then Father forbade me to jump the hedgerow. He said I was too young and inexperienced to take such chances. So I decided to prove that I wasn't too young, or too inexperienced."

"Was that when you had your accident?"

Mariah nodded. "I told Charles that I wanted to race him to the stream. He told me no. He said it was too far, that we'd have to jump the hedgerow, and Father told him not to let me jump it.

I gave in and told him we'd only race as far as the big tree before the hedgerow. He finally agreed, but when we got to the big tree, I didn't stop. I continued down the hill, and Charles followed. He kept up with me and jumped over the hedgerow the same time I did."

She pulled her hand out from beneath Jonah's. "I don't know how it happened, but in the middle of the jump, our horses collided. Charles and I both went to the ground, and our horses landed on top of us. I remember looking over at Charles and seeing him covered in blood. I thought he was dead."

Mariah rose and took several steps away from Jonah. "I don't know what happened after that. The next I knew, I was in my room and Mother was holding my hand. The doctor had been called, but he was with Charles. I was in great pain, but everyone was more concerned about Charles. I heard him tell Father that he doubted Charles would survive.

"Father was terribly angry with Charles. He told him that he'd refused to allow Charles to let me jump that hedgerow, but he'd allowed me to jump it anyway. I remember trying to tell Father that the accident was my fault, but I was so weak I couldn't say the words."

"Is that when you started giving Charles laudanum?"

"Soon after, yes. He needed it for the pain."

"What about you?"

"My pain receded within a few days. It wasn't until later that something happened. One night I doubled over in pain. It was the most stabbing pain I'd ever experienced, and I started to bleed."

"You were hemorrhaging," Jonah finished for her.

"Yes. That's what the doctor called it. He told Mama that he didn't think he could save me. There was only one thing he knew to do to help me, but he wasn't sure it would work. Mama told him to do whatever he had to in order to make the bleeding stop."

Mariah slowly turned to face Jonah. He'd lowered his head and dropped his face to his hands. He knew what the doctor was going to try to do. He knew what Mariah was going to say next.

"I was so glad to see you when you returned. It had been so long. But I knew from that first night that things could not be the same as before you left. I meant it when I told you that I loved you. I do, Jonah. But we can never act on that love."

"Mariah—"

"Shh," she said, then turned her back to him. "You told me your brother only asked one thing of you—to provide an heir so your family name didn't die out."

"Mariah—"

She held up her hand to stop his words and shook her head. "I can't give you that heir. I can't give you children."

"You don't know that," he said adamantly.

"Yes, I do. I haven't had my monthly courses since the accident. You're a doctor. You know what that means."

"Stop it, Mariah. You don't know what you're saying."

"Yes, I do. I know exactly what I'm saying. I'll help you find a perfect wife. One that can give you many babies. But that wife isn't me."

Jonah clasped his hands around her shoulders. "You're working yourself up for nothing, Mariah. I've already found the perfect wife. I found you."

"Except I can't give you what you want or what you need, Jonah."

"Then the Darbringth name will die out. I can live without the family name, Mariah. But I can't live without you."

She knew he meant what he said today, but he would regret his words tomorrow. He would regret his words when his brother hated him for choosing her over their family name. He would regret his decision when it was too late to make a different choice. No, she couldn't let him choose her when she couldn't give him the heir he needed.

Mariah swore she wouldn't cry. She swore she'd keep her emotions in check. But focusing on the pained expression on Jonah's face tore at her resolve until it was shredded. "Jonah, please. Don't make this any more difficult than it already is," she begged as the first tears streamed down her cheeks. "The fact is that we can't marry. You may love me today, but that love will turn to regret when you realize all you've given up to make me your wife."

"I don't care what I have to give up, Mariah. I can give up anything as long as you love me."

"No!" Mariah cried. "Just consider what you're saying, Jonah. You'd have to give up everything: a family, children, a brother. You know he would turn his back on you because you wouldn't do the one thing he asked of you. And all because of me." Mariah stepped out of his grasp and separated herself from him. "Even if you think you can make that choice, I can't let you."

"You can't stop me."

"Yes, I can. I can refuse to marry you. And I will."

The stricken look on Jonah's face tore at her. It ripped her heart from her breast to watch him.

"We need to retire," she said. "Tomorrow will be a long day, and you need your rest."

"No, Mariah. We can't leave this like it is. We need to work this out."

"There's nothing to work out, Jonah. I've known what I had to do from the moment you walked back into my life."

"Mariah!"

"No, Jonah. Nothing can come of our feelings."

Tears filled her eyes and streamed down her face as she hurried away from him.

So this is what it feels like when your heart breaks.

CHAPTER ELEVEN

I T WAS NO use trying to talk Mariah out of her decision to give him up. Jonah knew that. She'd struggled with what she was convinced she had to do since the night he walked back into her life. She didn't think she had a choice but to leave him, but he refused to accept that. There had to be an alternative. He couldn't give her up. His life wouldn't be worth living if she wasn't a part of his future.

"You're terribly quiet, Jonah," Jack said as they traveled to the Angel's Wings Orphanage. He and Charles and Jack rode together in one carriage, and Mariah and Annie rode in a second one. Jonah hoped that Annie could lighten Mariah's mood by the time they arrived at the orphanage.

He knew Mariah wasn't excited about going there, and he didn't blame her. What woman who couldn't have children could be excited about being surrounded by dozens of children who didn't have mothers?

"I didn't sleep well last night," he answered.

"I thought as much," Charles said. "I heard you come up the stairs shortly after Mariah."

Jonah raked his hands through his hair. "We had a discussion."

"Anything I should know about?" Charles asked with a serious expression on his face. "As her brother, that is?"

"When there is," Jonah said, dropping his head back against the leather cushion, "I'll let you know."

"You know, I thought I'd finally met the man for whom Mariah would give up the ridiculous notion that she didn't want to marry and settle down. But maybe she's more serious than I thought."

"Oh, she's serious," Jonah said, looking out the window. "But I'm not done trying to convince her that remaining single would be a tragic mistake."

"I wish you all the luck in the world, then, Jonah. There's no one I'd rather see her marry than you."

Just then, the carriage turned down the lane and stopped in front of the Angel's Wings Orphanage and Foundling Home. Jack exited first, and Charles and Jonah followed.

"Welcome!" a tall, broad-shouldered man said, rushing to meet Jack, then greeting him in an enthusiastic hug.

"Theo, you remember Jonah, don't you?" Jack asked.

"Of course!" Jonah said as he and Theo shook hands. "And this is Charles, Earl of Aspen."

"Just Charles." Charles and Theo shook hands.

When Jonah looked to the second carriage, he saw that Annie and Mariah had already disembarked.

The excitement was palpable. Jonah stepped over to Mariah and helped with the introductions. Theo and Livie accepted Mariah as if they'd known her for years instead of only minutes. When Charles and Mariah had been introduced to everyone, they entered the orphanage and were shown to a receiving room.

"You've made several improvements to the orphanage, Livie," Jack said when they entered an enlarged and newly decorated receiving room.

"It's amazing the changes and improvements you can make when you have more money," Livie said. "Especially when there are so many improvements to be made."

"I'm so glad you came to spend the day with us," Theo said. "Livie was especially looking forward to your visit. She spends so much time with the children that she longs for adult company."

"I wish I could say Theo is exaggerating, but unfortunately he isn't," Livie said, and everyone laughed. "I get so used to talking to the little ones that I find myself automatically looking down. Just this morning Theo asked me a question as he walked into the office and when I looked down, he said, 'Up here, sweetheart.'"

That brought forth a roar of laughter.

"We're going to have to make sure Livie only talks to adults all day," Annie said.

"That will be a treat, won't it, sweetheart?" Theo said, putting his arm around Livie's shoulders.

"Yes. It most certainly will," she said warmly, and looked at her husband with adoration in her eyes. "Now, let's sit down and enjoy some toast and pastries Mrs. Barnes baked for us, as well as some of our Angel's Wings jams and jellies. I hear Charles is dying to try them."

"I am," Charles said eagerly.

"Follow me, then, and we'll have a light repast."

Livie led the way to a formal dining room.

"It's too bad Quinn and Cassie couldn't join us," Jack said when they all reached the dining room. "Then you could have met all of us."

"How did you become acquainted?" Mariah asked.

"We served in the Crimean War together. When the war was over, Her Majesty's Special Forces had need for our services, so we worked for Her Majesty."

"Actually," Theo said with a smile, "Her Majesty had need of Quinn's services, and he only agreed to work as a special agent if the commanders signed Jack and me on, too."

"He was that good?" Charles asked.

Theo and Jack exchanged glances, then answered in unison. "He was."

"I look forward to meeting him," Charles said, admiration already evident in his tone.

"You are in for a big surprise, then," Theo said. "Because

Quinn and Cassie just happen to be here at this very moment."

Just then, the door to the dining room opened and a tall, imposing gentleman entered with a very pretty woman on his arm.

"Quinn!"

Jack strode to his friend and embraced him in a zealous hug. Jonah shook his hand, and introductions were made all around.

"Did you bring your children with you?" Annie asked after several servants brought in tea and trays of pastries and breads, and every different variety of jams and jellies.

"I suggested leaving them home," Cassie said. "But Quinn said everyone would want to see the children as much as they wanted to see us."

"You have to agree," Jack said with a smile on his face. "Having three boys who look alike is a rarity. Can you tell them apart yet, Quinn?"

"Finally," Quinn said on a laugh. "It was really embarrassing that I couldn't recognize my own children, especially when Cassie could tell them apart from the very beginning."

"Well, she's their mother," Annie said. "Mothers can always recognize their children."

Jonah only listened to the conversation going on around them with half an ear. The other half of his interest was concentrated on Mariah and her reaction to the constant talk about babies and families. She wore a smile and pretended interest in every word that was being said, but her face had lost its color long ago, and she had her hands clenched in her lap so tightly that her fingers were white.

"Would you care to take a walk around the garden, Mariah? I could stand to stretch my legs. I'm terribly stiff from riding and sitting."

"Of course," she said.

Jonah saw the relief on her face and hoped she only thought he needed her assistance, and not that she saw through his ruse to help her escape the talk of babies.

He rose, then extended his arm for her to take. "If you will excuse us," he said.

"Of course," everyone chorused.

Jonah and Mariah walked to the doors that led out onto the terrace, then proceeded down the steps and onto the path that meandered through the garden.

"Thank you," she said.

"It is I who should thank you," he insisted. "The muscles in my legs were cramping fiercely."

"And you could tell a voice inside my head was screaming for some excuse to get out of there."

"I thought perhaps we both needed a reason to leave," he said with a smile.

"It's too bad that we understand each other so completely," Mariah said. "That will be one of the characteristics I will search for when hunting for the perfect wife for you to marry."

"Stop, Mariah. You will not hunt for any such thing. I told you I have already found the woman I want to marry, and she is walking beside me right now."

"Jonah, please listen to me."

"Not if you are going to continue to talk such nonsense."

"I am only saying what we both must eventually face. You have no choice but to marry, and you can never marry me."

"I will concede a few of the points you've made. First, I do have to marry. But my main reason for marrying is that I don't want to live my life alone. I want to have someone to come home to at night. Someone with whom to talk over my day. And someone to wake up next to each morning and count my blessings because she is the only person whose face I want to see beside me.

"The second reason I want to marry is because I have been blessed enough to have given half my heart to the woman I love, and she has given me half of her heart in return."

"Oh, Jonah," Mariah said in a thick voice. "You have omitted the third reason."

"There is no third reason, Mariah."

"Children, Jonah. You forgot the children you want. The children you need."

"I will admit that I would love to have children, but only if God provides them." He stopped and faced her. "I do not need children, Mariah. Russell is in need of children. He is the one who is desperate to have an heir. I am not. I am only desperate to marry the love of my life."

"And if she will not marry you?"

"Then I will remain unmarried until she changes her mind."

Mariah's eyes filled with tears, and Jonah knew how much her heart ached. He knew how conflicted she was. She'd always done what was best for everyone else. She'd taken care of Charles. And she took care of *him*. Especially when Ralph Watson had nearly beaten him to death. Now, she was taking care of him by refusing to marry him. She thought it was the only way to protect him. But it wasn't.

Jonah pressed his finger beneath her chin and lifted her head. With the pads of his thumbs, he gently wiped away the tears that ran down her cheeks. "Mariah, I love you. I love only you."

And he lowered his head and kissed her.

Jonah was afraid she'd refuse his kisses, but she didn't. She accepted him with a desperation that filled his heart to overflowing.

He deepened his kisses, and she met each demand with a passion that mirrored his own. He kissed her again, then again, until it was difficult for either of them to breathe.

Jonah ended their kiss on a deep sigh, then wrapped his arms around her and nestled her close to him.

"Deny what our kisses make you feel if you can, Mariah. Deny that I possess your heart, if you can."

"I can't, Jonah. You know I can't. But neither can I marry you and ruin every chance for you to provide your family with the heir they need to keep the Darbringth line alive."

He clenched his jaw, disturbed by a twinge of anger. That

was not a choice for her to make.

Jonah held her close for a long while. He never wanted to let her go. He was afraid if he did, he might never get her back. And he wasn't sure he could survive if he lost her.

⊱⟫⟪⊰

WHEN THEY RETURNED to the house, the couples were deep in discussion. As soon as she and Jonah sat down, they were immediately included in the conversation.

"We were just talking about how we met the men we married. I know you're not married to Jonah, but it's obvious that you've known each other quite a while," Livie said. "How did you meet?"

"Well, we were neighbors," Mariah explained. "We grew up near each other."

She would have stopped there, but Jonah took over. "Not only did we grow up next to each other, but I used to visit Charles nearly every day, and Mariah would tag along with us wherever we went. She was in love with me even then."

Everyone laughed at the admission, especially when Mariah's face turned red.

"Well, you were," Jonah teased. "You've told me so."

"So, when is the wedding?" Quinn asked.

"I'm just waiting for Mariah to say yes," Jonah answered, and everyone cheered raucously and encouraged her to answer in the affirmative.

Mariah could have fallen through the floor if a hole had opened up, but of course, it didn't. Instead, she had to sit there and listen as the other couples revealed how they'd met. Thankfully, the subject eventually changed, and Quinn, Jack, and Theo talked about their time in the service together. It was obvious that they had done much good for Her Majesty's army.

"Did you all leave the force when you married?" Mariah

asked.

"We did," Quinn, Theo, and Jack answered together.

"We found it more important to stay with our wives and raise our children than risk going on a mission and not staying alive long enough to see our children grow up," Quinn said.

"Do you ever regret your decisions?" Mariah asked.

"Never," the three men answered. Jack continued, "If you listen to your heart, you'll never go wrong. It will tell you what to do every time."

Jonah's gaze locked with Mariah's. It was obvious that he hoped she had listened to Jack's words. That he hoped her heart was telling her that he couldn't live without her.

At last, everyone was ready to take a tour of the orphanage, and they rose from the table. They toured the schoolrooms where the children sat at their desks and learned their lessons.

"Where do these children go when they are too old to stay at Angel's Wings? I've noticed there aren't any older children here," Mariah said.

"There is a school in London that takes them," Livie replied. "Once there, they work in a variety of occupations, from being footmen, to stable hands, to lady's maids, to governesses, and anything in between. Then, at the end of a year, they choose what occupation they want to be trained in and start their apprenticeship."

"That sounds remarkable," Mariah said.

"It is. We've had a most gratifying success rate."

"And this," Theo said, placing his hand on one of the boy's shoulders, "is our son Jamie."

"Oh, we would never have guessed," Jack said, and everyone roared. He looked so much like Theo that it was possible to see what Theo must have looked like as a youngster.

Next, they went through to the nursery, where the small children ages two through four played with toys and balls. There were six children in this room, four little boys and two little girls.

Mariah struggled with a pain that formed in her breast. The little ones in this room were all adorable, and although they seemed happy and healthy, she knew they were alone. They were without parents to love them.

As if Jonah understood what she was feeling, he stepped up beside her and wrapped his arm around her waist, then pulled her close to him. It was amazing how he always knew what she was feeling. How he instinctively understood when she needed his closeness.

Finally, they went to the room where the babies slept. "We have six babes at present," Livie explained. "The youngest is only three days old and the oldest nearly a year old."

"How long will they stay here?" Mariah asked, stepping close to the cradles where the younger babes lay.

"Until they turn two years of age," Livie said. "Then they move on to the next room. Or they hopefully get adopted," she added.

"Do they all get adopted?" Mariah asked.

Jack and Livie exchanged looks filled with sadness. "Not all of them," Livie said as she shook her head. "Although the babies have the best chance of being adopted."

Mariah's face lost much of its color, and she clutched her hands to her waist as if fighting a sharp pain.

"It's all right, Mariah," Jonah whispered, tightening his grasp on her to hold her steady.

"What will happen to them then?"

"Like I explained earlier, they will stay here," Livie said. "They will be raised here and be educated here. When they are old enough to be trained in an occupation, they will graduate to another level and learn a skill. Then we will find them work, either on a farm, working as a laborer, or in one of the townhouses in London. Some of them go on to work in a shop. Some of them will work in our London jelly shop, and those who want to work as domestic servants will find positions in a townhouse in London. But we make sure all our children are trained in an occupation of their choice and find employment."

"But the babies," Mariah whispered, soft enough that only Jonah heard. "The babies."

CHAPTER TWELVE

M ARIAH STEPPED CLOSE to a cradle where one of the smaller babies lay. It was a little girl Mariah guessed was about six months old.

"Her name is Allison," Livie said, coming up beside her.

"Will she get adopted?"

"Perhaps. We can always hope she will," Livie said. "Although she'd have a better chance of finding a family if she were a boy."

Livie answered Mariah's frown with a smile. "Boys are in greater demand. They're needed to help on the farms. Girls aren't nearly as valuable."

"Oh," Mariah said, then reached out her finger and the baby clasped it. "She's strong for being so young."

"Yes," Livie agreed. "Would you like to hold her?"

"May I?"

"Of course." Livie lifted baby Allison from the cradle and placed her in Mariah's arms.

The bonding was immediate, and Mariah wanted to hold her close and never put her down.

"You can stay here as long as you like," Livie said as she turned to leave the room. "I'm going to show the others the rest of the orphanage, then I'll take them to the area where we make our jams and jellies." Livie shifted her gaze to Jonah. "You know where that is, Jonah. Bring Mariah there when she's ready to leave."

"Very well, Livie," he said.

After Livie left the room, Jonah led Mariah to a rocking chair, and she sat.

The baby had been sleeping, but when Mariah sat, she woke. Mariah was afraid she would cry, but she didn't. She opened her eyes and looked at Mariah, then smiled.

Mariah's eyes filled with tears, and Jonah wrapped an arm around her shoulders and knelt beside the rocker. She leaned into him, and for a few marvelous moments she allowed herself to pretend they were a family. That she finally possessed the one thing she'd always dreamed of having: a man who loved her and a baby of her own.

"I can give you the life you've always dreamed of, Mariah. That life can be yours."

Mariah stiffened, rose from the rocking chair, and placed the babe back in her cradle. "Yes, you could, Jonah. All you'd have to do is destroy the Darbringth name and ruin your family's lineage. Then I could watch you slowly hate yourself for refusing to do the one thing your brother requested you do, then come to hate me because I had destroyed everything that was expected of you."

She placed a blanket over the baby and turned toward the door. "I'd like to see where they make the jams and jellies. Will you take me?"

Jonah caught up with her and led her to the room off the kitchen where the work was done.

Mariah's heart had shattered when she held the babe and allowed herself to pretend, just for a moment, that the child was hers. That she could be a mother.

But that was something she must stop herself from imagining. That was something that could never be. That was a life she would never have.

⇾⇾⇾⇽⇽⇽

WATCHING MARIAH INTERACT with everyone as if she couldn't be happier tore at Jonah's insides. She was hurting and doing everything she could to hide it.

"Have you started making more jams and jellies?" she asked when she saw the stacks of empty jars ready to be filled.

"Not yet, but it won't be long. The strawberries are starting to ripen, and the other fruits won't be far behind," Livie answered.

"You have to write down the address of your shop in London so I can visit when we get back to Town," Mariah said.

"I will," Livie replied. "You can tell me what you think of it. Maybe give me a few suggestions on how to make it more attractive."

"I'm sure it's perfect," Mariah said cheerfully.

Jonah wanted to shake her. He wanted to tell her he knew her humor was an act, that she was aching inside and the last thing she wanted to do was laugh and pretend everything was perfect.

"I think the men went out to look at the berry hedgerows," Livie said. "They're massive. Would you like to see them? We can take a tour of the garden."

"We'd love to," the ladies said, and followed Livie out the workroom door.

Before Mariah could join them, Jonah reached out and stopped her from leaving. "Stop it, Mariah. You don't need to pretend that seeing the children didn't bother you. I know it did. You don't need to pretend that an orphanage isn't the last place you wanted to visit. I know it is."

He backed her up against a wall and stepped so close to her that there was barely any room separating them. He bracketed his arms on either side of her and trapped her next to the wall.

"Don't, Jonah."

"Don't what?"

He lowered his head, and she turned her face away from him.

"*Don't*," she repeated.

"Don't what?"

"You know," she said, then met his lips as he kissed her. Her passion was evident. Her desire was palpable. She wanted him as desperately as he wanted her. There was nothing either of them wanted more than to be in each other's arms, and showing each other how much they cared for one another.

Jonah deepened his kisses. He demanded more from her, and she gave it freely, willingly.

He opened his mouth atop hers, and she followed his lead. She allowed him to breech her lips and skim his tongue against the roof of her mouth, then against her lower lip. Her breathing came in harsh gasps as did his.

When Jonah could breathe no longer and Mariah struggled to catch her own breath, he broke their kiss and brought her close to him.

"This doesn't mean anything, Jonah," she whispered on a harsh gasp. "We'll always lust for one another, but that is the end of it."

"Bloody hell. You can lie to yourself all you want, Mariah, but it doesn't hide the truth. Our kisses mean a hell of a lot more than lust. Our kisses mean that I can't get along without you and you can't survive without me. Our kisses prove just how much we love each other."

He wrapped his arms around her and cradled her next to him. He didn't want to release her. He wanted to keep her next to him forever.

She wrapped her arms around his waist and buried her face against his chest. "I need to leave. I need to join the rest of the ladies. If I don't return soon, Charles will come looking for me."

"Let him find you, Mariah. Then he'll force you to marry me."

Mariah pushed herself away from Jonah. She shook her head,

telling him she couldn't allow that to happen.

He watched her nearly run away from him, watched her leave through the back door and walk toward the hedgerows loaded with berries. He followed her, but stopped when she did. Her head dropped to her hands and her shoulders shook with emotion.

He wanted to gather her in his arms. He wanted to comfort her and tell her that everything would be all right, but at that moment he knew that nothing would ever be right again.

Mariah was correct. They couldn't marry. He had an obligation to Russell. He had an obligation to his family, to the Darbringth title. And he couldn't walk away from that obligation the same as he'd walked away from his family when he decided to become a doctor.

Jonah clutched his hand to his chest. His heart hurt more than it had ever ached before. He'd been selfish when he put his own desires ahead of what his father wanted for him. He'd put himself ahead of any family obligation when he'd left to become a doctor and hadn't returned even when his father was sick and dying.

He couldn't put himself ahead of what Russell was asking of him now. Being so selfish would, at the very least, cause the Darbringth dynasty to die out—at the worst, cost Russell's wife her life if she went against the doctor's advice and risked another pregnancy.

Either way, Jonah had always been a self-centered, heartless bastard who didn't deserve someone as noble and self-sacrificing as Mariah. The only thing he'd done by pursuing her was to cause her immense pain. She was correct. He had no choice but to return to London and find a wife who could give him the heirs he needed to save his family's title.

That didn't mean he would ever love anyone other than Mariah. He wouldn't. He couldn't. She possessed his heart, and there wasn't enough of it left to share with anyone else.

But he couldn't abandon his family. He couldn't deny the one request Russell had made of him.

Mariah had always known that.

He'd just figured that out.

"YOU ARE BEING very quiet," Annie said as she and Mariah rode back to Burnhaven. "Is something wrong?"

"I'm not sure," Mariah said, lowering her gaze to her hands clasped in her lap.

"Is it Jonah?"

Mariah lifted her watery gaze as the first tear spilled from her eye and ran down her cheek.

Annie slid across the carriage to sit beside Mariah. "You may as well tell me," she said, clasping Mariah's hands. "Because you know I'm not going to give up until I find out what's wrong."

Mariah swiped the tear from her face. "Jonah and I argued."

"About what?"

"Oh, Annie," Mariah said through her tears.

"He asked you to marry him, didn't he?"

Mariah heard the excitement in Annie's voice and knew she had to quell it. "Yes, but I told him I couldn't marry him."

Annie gasped. "Why, Mariah? It's obvious you two love each other. Anyone with eyes in their head can see you were made for each other."

"But we can't marry."

"Why? You two are perfect for each other."

"But we're not, Annie. I'm not perfect for Jonah."

"Please explain, Mariah, because I don't believe you."

Mariah wiped the tears from her face and took a deep breath before she started her explanation. That was the only way she'd get out the words she had to say. "One of the main reasons that Russell wrote to Jonah to ask him to return to London was so that he could find a wife to marry. Someone who could give him a son to carry on the Darbringth title."

Annie shook her head. "I don't understand, Mariah. Why doesn't that make you happy?"

"Because…" Mariah struggled to get the words out. "Because I can't give him the children he needs, Annie. I'm barren."

"You can't know that, Mariah," Annie huffed. "Many women think they are barren, then, when they least expect it, they discover they're pregnant."

"That won't be me, Annie. I was in a severe riding accident when I was sixteen. I haven't had my courses since then. I can't have children."

Annie couldn't speak for several long moments. "Does Jonah know that?"

"Yes. He knows."

"What did he say?"

"He told me he didn't care. He said that he loves me and refuses to give me up. But that was last night."

"And now?"

"He came to me as we were getting ready to leave and told me that I was right. He thanked me for refusing to marry him and for demanding that he do the right thing for his family."

"Oh, Mariah," Annie said. "I'm sorry."

"Don't be, Annie. This is the way I knew it had to be."

"What are you going to do now?"

"When we return to Hope's House, Charles and I will pack our belongings and return to London. As soon as we get there, I'll begin my search for the perfect wife for Jonah. My sister still attends all of Society's events. I'll find the perfect wife for Jonah, and make sure he marries before the Season comes to an end."

Annie reached for Mariah's hands and gave them a comforting squeeze. "And you. Will *you* be all right?"

"Yes, Annie. I'll be fine. I've always known that marriage was not in my future. I just forgot for a few moments and imagined that I could have the man of my dreams."

"You *found* the man of your dreams," Annie said on a heavy sigh. "It's just that your dream didn't last into the future."

➤➤➤◄◄◄

"WHAT ARE YOU doing?" Jonah asked from the doorway to Mariah's room.

Bony fingers of dread clamped around Mariah's heart and squeezed until she had a difficult time breathing. She hadn't heard him approach her room, and he startled her. "Packing."

"Why?"

She had hoped he wouldn't notice that she was leaving until the last moment and she was on her way to the carriage. "Charles and I are leaving."

"Why?"

"It's time, Jonah. Charles is anxious to return to London, and so am I."

"Were you going to tell me goodbye?"

"Yes, Jonah," she answered, but the look on his face indicated he wasn't sure she was telling him the truth.

She put the last of her incidentals into a small leather case and lowered the lid. Even though she tried to keep her hands steady, they shook so violently that she could barely control them. Her nerves were getting the better of her.

"What do you intend to do when you get to London?"

"I will resume my duty to my sister and chaperone her to the events she wishes to attend. Hopefully, she'll be able to announce her engagement by the end of the Season and we can begin to plan a wedding. And," she said, lifting her gaze to meet his, "I intend to search for a suitable wife for you."

Jonah spun from her and slammed his fist against the door frame. "Bloody hell, Mariah!" He spun back and glared at her. "I don't need anyone to help me find a wife. Especially you!"

"I'm only trying to help, Jonah."

"I don't need your help. I don't *want* your help!"

"I know you don't," she said softly. "But there might be a perfect candidate that you have overlooked, and I—"

"No! Stay the hell out of my life. You've done enough already."

Mariah lowered her gaze and focused on closing her small case. She wanted him gone before he saw the tears that threatened to fall.

"You aren't going to make this easy on me, are you, Mariah?"

She met his angry words with a hostile glare. "Easy on *you*? What do you think it's like for me?"

"I don't know. Did you ever care for me enough to try to find a solution to our problem?"

"There isn't a solution, Jonah. I've known that I couldn't marry since I was sixteen years old. I can't give you the one thing your family needs from you, and in time, you'd hate me for trapping you in a childless marriage."

Jonah turned away from her and braced his outstretched arms against the wall. He lowered his head and took in a deep breath. "You're right, Mariah. This is not your fault. It's no one's fault." He pushed himself away from the wall and turned to face her. "I'm sorry. You didn't deserve my wrath and temper. I apologize. Goodbye, Mariah. Have a good life."

And he turned and left her.

Mariah sat down on the edge of the bed and let the tears she'd kept bottled away flow freely. She didn't know how long she sat there before Charles entered the room.

"Are you ready to leave?" he asked.

"Yes," she answered. "I was just reliving all the experiences we had while we were here. Have I told you how proud I am of you?"

"Yes, Mari. You have. And I'm so glad you encouraged me to come. I feel like a new person. I could never have rid myself of my dependence on the drug if you hadn't helped me."

"This is our chance to start over, Charles. Let's do it up properly and make a success of our futures."

"Yes, let's," he said, then picked up her bag and escorted her to the carriage.

Although Mariah didn't expect Jonah to be there when they left, he was. He stood by the carriage as if he'd been waiting for them.

"Goodbye, Mariah," he said. He reached for her hands and held them. "Take care of yourself. You are a very special person."

She struggled to keep her voice steady, trying to hide the pain that stabbed through her heart. "You too, Jonah. I wish you all the best."

He held her hands a moment longer than was appropriate. It was as if he realized that once he released her, he would never see her again.

Their gazes locked, and Mariah fought to look away from him. This would no doubt be the last time they would speak.

That thought caused a lump to build in her throat, and she was forced to turn away from him and step into the carriage. She could only hold her composure for a few seconds more before she feared she would break down in front of him.

Mariah sat in the shadowed corner while Charles thanked Jonah and said his goodbyes. Before she was prepared to leave Jonah forever, the carriage lurched forward, and the horses carried them away from Hope's House.

"You love him," Charles said after they'd ridden in silence for several minutes. "It's plain for anyone to see. And he loves you. So why don't you do something about it?"

She turned her head and looked out the window, then gave it up to fumble for a somewhat dry handkerchief.

"Talk to me, Mari," he said, moving to sit next to her. "You've kept something trapped inside you for years. We've always shared everything." Charles reached for her hands and held them. "Share this with me. Let me help you like you've helped me with my opium issue."

She lifted one hand and dabbed at the tears running down her cheeks with her handkerchief.

"I know something's wrong, Mari. Why do you refuse every proposal of marriage laid at your feet? Why do you refuse to have what every other woman wants in her life—a home, a husband, children?"

"Because I can't, Charles. I can't have a home or a husband, because I can't give any man children."

"What do you mean?" he asked with a confused expression on his face.

"Exactly what I said. I can't give any man children. Because of the accident we had, I can't have children."

Charles looked at her for several long moments. His expression changed from concern to disappointment to remorse. "Oh, Mariah," he said on a heavy sigh.

"Yes, Charles. I can't give any man the one thing he wants: an heir to carry on the family name."

"And Jonah?"

"That's the one thing he needs from a wife, an heir to carry on the Darbringth title. His brother has four children, all girls, and his sister-in-law can't have more children. The doctor told her husband that going through another birth would probably kill her. So it's up to Jonah to provide an heir."

"I see."

"Yes."

"I'm sorry, Mariah."

"Don't be, Charles. I've always known I would never marry."

Her brother wrapped his arm around her shoulder and pulled her next to him. Mariah laid her head on her brother's chest and felt the comforting touch that he provided. It was almost reassuring and consoling as what she felt when Jonah held her.

Yet it wasn't.

No man's hold could ever be as reassuring as when Jonah held her.

CHAPTER THIRTEEN

JONAH HAD SEVERAL new patients that he felt obligated to help before he could return to London. It wasn't that his associates couldn't handle them. They could. It was more that he didn't have the courage to return just yet. Not while Mariah was attending Society's balls and soirees with her sister in tow.

He knew that Russell would want him to attend those same events, and if he did, he would very likely run into Mariah while he was there. He was afraid his heart couldn't survive the pain of seeing her at every turn without being able to hold her, or talk to her, or kiss her.

He tried not to think about her every moment of every day and every night, but it was impossible. As long as he kept busy during the day, and kept himself occupied with his work, he could manage to a certain degree, but nights were impossible.

The second he laid his head on his pillow, she appeared in his mind. Her face appeared in front of him, and he couldn't make it go away. Her smile haunted him, and her voice echoed in his ears. Everything about her pursued him and wouldn't release him from her spell. He loved her. He'd spent his life searching for someone just like her. But that mythical creature did not exist.

Jonah went through his routine. He checked on his patients and evaluated their advancements. He went through their progress reports and wrote down instructions for the attendants.

He was running out of projects that would keep him from returning to London, whether he was ready to face Mariah or not.

He finished his paperwork and looked up when there was a knock on the door. "Yes."

"This just arrived for you from London, Dr. Reynolds. The messenger came in a carriage with instructions to wait for you."

One of his assistants held out a message, and Jonah took it. It was from Russell.

Jonah—Come as soon as you can. It's important.

R

"I've been called to London," he said, rising to his feet. "You know how to reach me should you need me."

"Yes, Dr. Reynolds."

Jonah went to his rooms, packed his clothes in a trunk, and within an hour he was in the carriage and on the road to London.

Something was wrong. Russell would not have sent such an urgent message if it wasn't serious. Jonah only wished his brother had given him a hint as to what the problem was. Was Russell ill? Was it one of the children? Was it Julia?

Or was it Mariah?

A knot formed in his stomach. He would hate for it to be any of those dreaded possibilities—but the worst would be if it were Mariah. He prayed it wasn't her.

Her face appeared before him. Her smile. The color of her hair. The sound of her voice. Anyone but Mariah.

Anyone but Mariah.

THE HOURS IT took to make his way to London were the longest of his life. Even though the driver made good time, Jonah doubted they'd ever arrive, but as nightfall approached, the carriage pulled up before Darbringth House.

Jonah jumped to the ground and raced up the walk. The door opened before he could knock, and Julia met him. Thankfully, she looked healthy and well.

"Jonah, what a surprise! I didn't expect you."

He gave his sister-in-law a hug in greeting. "How are you, Julia? Is everyone well?"

"Yes. We're all just fine. Were you worried over us?"

"No," he lied. "It's just been so long since I've last seen you."

"Yes, it has. Russell was just commenting that he wondered when you would be returning. I think he missed you."

"I missed him too."

"We've seen Mariah at several of Society's events over the last few weeks."

"Is she well?"

"Yes, she seemed quite well the last time I saw here. Not as happy as when she was with you, Jonah. But physically well."

"Good," he said. "Is Russell in?"

"Yes. He's in the study. Would you like me to take you in to see him?"

"No, I can find my way."

Jonah gave Julia a kiss on the cheek, then made his way to Russell's study. When he reached the room, he knocked, then opened the door.

"Yes?"

Jonah entered and looked at Russell. He looked terrible. His face was pale, his features were drawn, and there were dark circles beneath his eyes.

"What is it, Russell? Are you ill?"

"No, it's not me."

"Then who?"

"It's Julia."

"I just saw her. She said she was fine."

"But she's not. She's pregnant."

"What?"

"She's expecting a baby. She saw the doctor, and he confirmed it. She's pregnant."

"How did that happen?"

Russell looked at him as if he had two heads. "You know how it happens, Jonah. Don't tell me I need to explain it to you."

"Of course I know *how* it happens, but you said—"

"I know what I said, but—"

"Never mind," Jonah interrupted, then poured himself a glass of brandy and sat in a chair in front of Russell's desk. "This is a catastrophe. What are you going to do?"

Russell lifted his tear-filled gaze. "Pray, Jonah. I don't have any other choice." He took a swallow from his glass. "And now I have another favor to ask. An even bigger favor."

Jonah kept his gaze focused on his brother.

"I don't trust any of the doctors in London to keep Julia alive. I want you to be with Julia when she has her baby. If anyone can get her through the delivery, it's you."

"Delivering babies isn't my specialty, Russell."

"If something happens during the birth, I want you to be with us. I trust you, and I know you'll do everything possible to save Julia's life."

"Of course I will." Jonah took another swallow of his liquor. "Does Julia know the risks of having another babe?"

"Yes. The doctor told her."

"How did she take the news?"

"She laughed at him. She told him she wasn't worried. Everything would be all right. And maybe this time she'd give me a boy."

"Maybe she will," Jonah replied, trying to keep his voice light.

"I don't care if she has a boy or a girl, as long as Julia survives the birth."

"We'll hope for that. Whatever happens, it's out of our hands now. Only God knows what will happen."

Before Jonah left, there was a knock on the door and Julia entered. Both men stood.

"Please, stay seated," she said. She walked over to her husband and placed her hand on Russell's shoulder. "Did Russell tell you our exciting news?"

"Yes," Jonah answered with as much enthusiasm as he could muster. "Congratulations!"

"Thank you," she said, sitting on Russell's lap when he wrapped his arm around her waist and pulled her down to him.

"What did the doctor tell you?"

"The same as always. That I should get plenty of rest and not overdo."

Jonah kept his gaze focused on Julia. "I think it is something we should keep in mind. How do you feel?"

A smile lit her face. "Excited, Jonah. Maybe this time it will be a boy."

"Yes, maybe it will."

"But I'll be happy if it's another girl. As long as it's healthy."

"Yes, that's the main thing. How many menses have you missed?"

"This month is the fourth."

"So, your baby should arrive in five months."

"Yes. Isn't that exciting?" she said.

Russell and Jonah agreed in unison, but neither of them were at all convincing.

Julia rose from Russell's lap. "Are you going to accompany us to the Packworth ball tonight? I'd like to go, since I won't be able to attend many more social events before I'm too large to be seen in public."

Jonah considered if he wanted to attend a ball. He'd just arrived in London. He really wanted to stay in and rest, and yet, perhaps Mariah would be there, and he would have an opportunity to speak to her. At least he'd be able to see her.

"Yes, I think perhaps I will accompany you. But I don't intend to stay late. And neither will you. I'll be your watchdog to make sure you don't overdo it. And you will do as I say, young lady. By the time this baby makes an appearance, you'll want me to return to Hope's House and leave you in peace."

The couple laughed at his joke, except Russell and Jonah knew it wasn't a joke, but a very serious promise.

MARIAH SAT AGAINST the wall at the Packworth ball and watched Felicity dance her second dance with the Earl of Pembleton. Charles had stopped by earlier and told her that Pembleton had asked to speak with him tomorrow. Mariah was glad. This would finally be over. Felicity would be engaged, and they could start planning a wedding. Then Mariah would be finished in London and could return to the country. She was looking forward to that day.

She thought of the months she'd spent in London and couldn't wait for some peace and quiet. She'd been forced to attend more balls and musicales than she'd ever attended in her life. At least she was here alone. At least Jonah wasn't here to remind her of the life that was possible with him at her side. At least Jonah wasn't here to stir her heart to a fevered pitch.

Thankfully, he had been kind enough to stay away from London for the last several weeks. If he did return, it wouldn't be for long. The Season was almost over.

Mariah shifted her gaze from Felicity and Lord Pembleton to Charles and the female with whom he was dancing. She couldn't believe how he had changed since they'd returned to London. He had transformed from an aloof lord who failed to interact with any of the females of the *ton* to one of the most sought-after men with a title. His personality had changed from recluse to one of the most outgoing men in London. There was a never-ending stream of invitations that arrived each and every day for him.

She was glad. She wanted him to find someone to marry and be happy with.

The dance ended, and Charles escorted his dance partner

back to her circle of friends, then looked up to the top of the stairs.

A wide grin lit his face, and he took the first steps to where a trio of late-arriving guests entered the ballroom.

Her heart leaped in her breast and began a thundering explosion when she saw the three newcomers. Russell greeted Charles as if they were long-lost friends who hadn't seen each other in months.

He then greeted Lord and Lady Darbringth, and finally he greeted Jonah.

Mariah's stomach churned, then did several somersaults before Jonah found her. It was as if he were purposely searching her out. Once he found her, Charles separated him from the other guests and ushered him over to where she stood.

She wasn't sure whether she wanted Jonah to greet her so they could pretend that they were remote acquaintances, or if she wanted him to stop to visit with other guests so she would have a chance to escape his notice and not have to suffer being close to him.

The choice, however, was taken out of her hands when Jonah came to her and planted himself just beyond the hem of her skirt.

"Good evening, Mariah," he greeted her, then took her hands and raised them to his lips.

"Good evening, Jonah."

"You're looking well," he said.

"As are you. I've been waiting for you to return to London."

"Yes. I received a note from Russell informing me that I was needed."

"Is everything well?"

"I'm not sure."

Mariah couldn't hide her frown.

"Would you care to walk in the garden?"

She cast a glance at Charles to tell him she would be back shortly, but he was surrounded by several couples, and would no doubt not even notice that she was gone.

Jonah held out his arm, and Mariah placed her fingers on his sleeve. They walked out the doors, across the terrace, then down the path that led through a clever arrangement of potted ornamental trees.

Walking with him, touching him, feeling the heat of his body through her clothing, caused the same sensation as it always did. She'd prayed that the time they were apart had changed their reaction to each other. But it hadn't.

"What's wrong, Jonah?" she asked when they were far enough out of range that they wouldn't be overheard.

"I would like to ask your help."

"Of course," she said, growing concerned. "What do you need me to do?"

He led her to a gazebo positioned on the side of the path, and they sat there together. "Do you remember when I told you that the doctor said it wasn't wise for Julia to become pregnant again?"

"Yes, you said his opinion was that he feared her heart would not be able to stand the strain of another pregnancy."

"Yes. Well, Russell called me home because Julia is pregnant again."

"Oh, no," she said, looking into Jonah's eyes. She could tell from the worry in his gaze that he was more than a little concerned. He was terrified. "You mentioned you wanted my help. What can I do?"

"I noticed that you and Julia got along quite well when I was here before. Would it be possible for you to spend some time with her on a regular basis?"

"Of course. I'd love to."

"What I intend to do is confine her to her bed in a few weeks. She will be quite bored when she can't get up and play with her girls. Since you are already aware of her condition, you will be able to watch her to make sure she doesn't overexert herself."

"Is she aware of the risks to her health?"

"The doctor told her what he always did—to get plenty of rest and drink plenty of liquids."

"But did you tell her what the risks are?"

Jonah didn't answer immediately. Instead, he focused on Mariah and shook his head.

"Are you going to tell her?"

"I think we should, but Russell is hesitant to say anything to her. He's afraid it will cause her too much anxiety."

"Doesn't he realize that if she is aware of the risks, she will take more care of herself and not overdo it?"

"He just doesn't want her to worry, but I hope to talk him out of that."

"Tell him that as soon as you confine her to her bed, she'll know something is wrong."

He smiled. "You're correct. I imagine every woman knows that."

"Yes, I imagine they do," she replied.

Mariah sat with Jonah for a few silent moments. It was so peaceful to be with him and not be forced to talk about anything in particular.

"How is Charles doing?" he said, breaking the silence.

"Remarkably well. He's gone to more balls and social events than ever, and has attracted quite a number of interested females."

"That's exactly what I'd hoped. Perhaps you'll have to plan more than one wedding in the future."

"I would enjoy that," she said with a smile on her face.

"Then what will you do when you get your siblings married off?"

"I will retire to the country and lead a quiet and serene life."

"Don't you think an uneventful life might be boring?"

"Perhaps," she said, shrugging her shoulders. "But I will welcome it. There's a great comfort in knowing tomorrow will be just like today." Mariah lifted her gaze and focused on Jonah. "What about you? Have you found anyone you wish to make your wife?"

"No, Mariah. If things go well with Julia, and she gives Russell his heir, I may not have to be in such a hurry to marry. I have a hospital to run and patients to cure."

"Jonah, don't live your life alone. Find someone to marry. Someone who can give you children. You have too much love to share. Don't be selfish with your love."

"What about you?"

"I'm a different story. I have nothing to give any man. But we've gone through this at great length. It will do no good to bring it up again."

Mariah lifted her gaze and looked up at the sky. It was a beautiful evening. The moon was full and surrounded by stars. "We should be getting back," she said. "We'll cause talk."

"Yes," Jonah said, getting to his feet.

"You'll tell me when I should begin visiting Julia more regularly."

"Yes. I'll let you know. Thank you, Mariah."

"Not at all. It will be my pleasure. I'll look forward to spending time with your lovely sister-in-law."

"She'll enjoy your company, too."

Mariah placed her hand on Jonah's sleeve, and they returned to the ballroom. Her heart beat faster in her breast as she remembered what it had been like the last time they were in a garden together. The last time he'd kissed her. She was glad he hadn't tonight, and yet…

…she would dream about his kisses and regret that he hadn't kissed her just one last time.

CHAPTER FOURTEEN

MARIAH APPROACHED THE countess's townhouse with a light step. This was the first time she had come to see Julia. Jonah had informed her that he'd ordered his sister-in-law to remain in bed for the remainder of her pregnancy and asked if she would come calling and spend a few hours with her. Of course, Mariah said yes. She knew how bored Julia must be just lying in bed with nothing to do.

The door opened before she reached for the knocker, and Jonah invited her in.

"Welcome, Mariah," he said, reaching for her hand. "Thank you for coming."

"It's my pleasure. How is your sister-in-law?"

"She's had some discomfort this past week, so I confined her to her bed. It's too early for the baby to arrive, so I insisted on bed rest to help her carry the babe as long as she can."

"How much longer are you hoping she can last before birthing her baby?"

"At least two months more. Three would be even better, but I don't think she'll make it that long."

"What makes you think that?"

"The doctor was correct when he advised Russell not to let his wife carry another babe. She isn't strong enough. It isn't just her heart that probably won't take the stress, but her body, too.

Having four babies so close together has weakened her muscles. I'm afraid she doesn't have the strength she'll need to birth a babe."

Mariah felt fierce waves of concern for Julia. There were always risks in childbirth, and it wasn't uncommon for a woman to not survive the ordeal. But the thought of losing Julia tore at Mariah's heart. She and Russell had four daughters who needed a mother to love them and raise them. There were four children, and possibly one more, who needed the nurturing that only a mother could provide. And if something happened to Julia, Mariah wasn't sure how Russell would cope. The love they possessed for each other was plain to see.

"I should go up to spend the afternoon with her," Mariah said, then turned toward the stairs.

Before she could ascend past the newel post, Jonah reached out and stopped her. His hand slid down her arm and his fingers twined with hers.

"Thank you, Mariah. I know it's not easy for you to be here."

"Just as it's not easy for you to have me here," she said, letting him hold her hand without pulling it away. She wanted the connection.

"No, it's not," he whispered, then released her hand.

Mariah clutched her trembling hands at her waist and walked up the stairs. She tried to calm her nerves before she entered Julia's room, but Jonah always affected her more than she wanted him to. It was a feeling she doubted would ever go away.

She knocked on the door and entered when Julia bade her to enter. "Good day, Julia," she said when she entered the room. "I came to visit. I hope you don't mind."

"Mariah," Julia greeted her. "Oh, I'm so glad you've come to call. I was about to sneak out of my room. Jonah has confined me to this bed, and I'm not sure I can take it."

Mariah sat in the chair next to the bed and handed Julia a small gift she'd brought her.

"Oh, you didn't have to bring me anything."

"It's a little something I made that I wanted you to have."

Julia opened the present and took out the set of embroidered handkerchiefs. "Oh, Mariah. They're beautiful."

"Thank you. I was in a similar situation after my accident and was not allowed to leave my bed. That's why I know how helpless you feel. My mother supplied me with a never-ending quantity of items to embroider. I swear embroidering each and every one of them was all that saved my sanity."

"I can see where having something to do would help pass the time. I will have to send one of the staff out to get me some handwork to embroider."

"And be sure to have a ready supply of books to read. You can only embroider so long, just as you can only read so long. Having a variety of projects to work on will help pass the time."

"Will you come as often as you can? Having someone to talk to will help, too. And it will keep my mind off whatever it is that Jonah and Russell are fearful of."

Mariah smiled, then patted Julia's hand. "I will make it a point to come nearly every day. That will give me something to do, too."

At that moment, a maid carried in a tea tray and set it on a nearby table. Mariah thanked the servant and poured tea then put a pastry on a plate and handed it to Julia.

"Has Jonah explained what has him concerned?" Mariah asked when she had her tea and pastry.

"No. But he and Russell have had several quiet conversations. I know they're discussing me and this pregnancy."

"That's no doubt true, because Jonah is a doctor and Russell wants to take advantage of his knowledge."

"No, there's something else. I thought Russell would be ec-static that I was pregnant again, but this is the first time that he almost appears to be angry because I'm going to have a baby."

"I'm sure he isn't angry," Mariah said, trying to comfort Julia. "He's no doubt just considering all the dowries he'll have to come up with if you have another girl."

"Oh, I sincerely hope that this time I'll give Russell a son. Even though he assures me he doesn't care if I give him another daughter, I know he'd rather have a son. He's anxious to have an heir."

"The world will not end if you have another daughter, Julia. There's always Jonah. I'm sure he'll find the perfect person to marry who will provide him with a Darbringth heir."

Julia finished her tea and set the saucer in her lap. Then she leveled on Mariah a forlorn expression. "Does that mean you're serious about never marrying, Mariah?"

Mariah fought that painful grip that tightened deep in her breast every time she was forced to admit that she would never find a man to love her. A man with whom she could make a family.

"I've always known it was impossible for me to marry, Julia. No matter what they say, there isn't a man alive who doesn't want to father his own children."

"Have you spoken with Jonah?"

Mariah tried to look unconcerned. "We've spoken, but have not come to an agreeable solution. We've exhausted the topic of marriage."

They talked companionably several minutes longer, but Mariah made sure to avoid the subject of marriage. There was no use in speaking about a topic that had already been beaten to death.

Just as she was about to tell Julia goodbye, there was a knock on the door and Jonah and Russell were there.

"Hello, ladies," Russell greeted them. "Have you had a pleasant afternoon?"

"It was wonderful," Julia said. "Look what Mariah brought for me."

She handed Russell the handkerchiefs Mariah had given her, and he and Jonah looked at them appreciatively. "That's beautiful work," Jonah said, locking his gaze with Mariah's.

"I told Julia that I've had a great deal of practice at embroidering. That's how I spent most of my time after my accident. By the time I was able to get out of bed, I'd embroidered so many handkerchiefs, everyone in my family begged me to stop giving them any more."

"You did a most admirable job, Mariah. You're quite accomplished."

"Thank you, Jonah. They are not that remarkable. You're just impressed because you didn't think I had any talents and I've surprised you."

Julia and Russell laughed while Jonah tried to take back his words and convince Mariah that he didn't mean that at all.

"Too late, Jonah," she teased. "I know what you meant."

Everyone had another good laugh. "It's time I left," she said, then leaned over the bed and kissed Julia's cheek. "Good day, Julia. I'll see you again tomorrow, if you'd like."

"I'd love for you to come again. Visiting with you made the day go ever so much faster."

Mariah gave Julia a comforting smile, then walked through the door that Jonah held for her.

"Thank you, Mariah," he said, escorting her down the stairs. "You were great for Julia's humor."

She didn't say anything until they reached the bottom of the stairs. Then she turned and faced him. "Your sister-in-law is not a shallow person, Jonah. She knows something is wrong. Something that neither you nor Russell are telling her. My advice is to tell her what that something is so she can face it squarely."

"What did she say to you?"

"Only that you and Russell are keeping something from her. This was the first time she told Russell that she was expecting a child and he wasn't thrilled. She said that you have been watching her like the proverbial mother hen and now she's confined to her bed. She knows something is wrong. Tell her."

Jonah took a step away from her, then turned to face her. "You're correct. Julia is not a fool. She knows something is amiss.

"Tell her what it is. She's strong enough to handle the news, and I'll be here to see her again tomorrow and talk her through her fears."

He reached for her hands and pulled her into his arms. This was the exact place she wanted to be, but this was the last place she could allow herself to be.

"I have to get home," she said, pulling away from him. "I am expected to accompany Felicity to the Wariner ball tonight."

"Perhaps I will see you then," Jonah said.

"Surely you are not going to allow Julia to attend any social events?"

"No," he said with a seductive grin on his face. "I'm supposed to be searching for someone to be my wife, am I not? Where better to be than where all the intended targets are gathered? Hm?"

"Don't expect me to fall for your tricks," she said. "I will not pay attention to you or your advances. Your goal is to find a wife, and I am not in the running. You would be better off spending your time here, speaking with your sister-in-law." Mariah turned her back on him and walked out the door.

Each time she was near him, her heart raced in her breast. Every time she was in his presence, she had to fight harder to ignore the pull his nearness had on her.

Mariah walked the four short blocks that separated the Aspen townhouse from the Darbringth townhouse. She needed the time to let her mind work out the problems she was facing.

"DID YOU KNOW the reason Jonah and Russell were so concerned about the baby?" Julia asked when Mariah was seated in the chair beside Julia's bed and had served tea.

Mariah took a sip of her tea. "Yes. I knew. Which is why I told Jonah to tell you about the problem."

"Thank you," Julia said. "I would much rather have known

than simply thinking that Jonah was being overprotective without cause."

"I know," Mariah agreed. "That's the way I felt when I discovered I couldn't have children. My parents tried to keep it from me at first, thinking to spare me. But when I had my first serious suitor, my mother realized she needed to tell me to break off the courtship because it wasn't right for me to lead him on when I couldn't provide him with an heir."

"I'm glad I know. It makes lying in bed ever so much easier when I know that I'm doing it for my baby, and not just to please Russell."

Mariah reached over and patted Julia's hand. "That's how I thought you would feel about it. I'm glad it was the right choice."

"So, I have some very difficult questions to consider. I'm hoping you can help me with them."

"I'll do what I can," Mariah said with a knot forming in the pit of her stomach. She knew what Julia was going to ask of her.

"If something happens to me—"

"No, we're not going to think that way," she said. "Nothing is going to happen to you."

"But if it does, would you consider taking my girls? I know it's a lot to ask, but I have no family left, and Jonah is Russell's only family. I need someone I can trust to raise them as I would want them raised, and you are the only person I trust enough to do that."

Mariah considered what Julia was asking of her and knew she couldn't say no, and yet it caused a chill to traverse her spine.

"I promise you that I will make sure your daughters are well taken care of, just as I know it will never come to that. You will survive this baby's birth the same as you have survived the last five babies' births. This one will be no different."

"I pray you are right. I would so like to see my children grow up and find husbands to love and take care of them."

"And you will."

Julia smiled with tears in her eyes. "Yes, I will," she answered in a shaky voice.

"Now," Mariah said, "what other concerns do you have? I'm sure there are many."

"Not so many. The children are my main concern. Oh, there's Russell, but I will talk to him before the time comes and tell him to help you and Jonah take care of the girls, and, when he's done missing me, that I won't blame him if he finds another person to love and marry. He has made me exceedingly happy. I would want him to share that love with someone else who deserves to find happiness."

"You are a remarkable woman, Julia. It's a good thing that you are going to come through this birth with no problems, so you can continue to be the recipient of Russell's love and attention for the rest of your life."

Julia patted Mariah's hand in a show of affection. "Now, Mariah. Did you bring me some embroidery to work on? I need to stay occupied while I lie in bed."

"As it so happens, I did," Mariah said, then pulled some work out of her small tapestry bag and handed it to Julia.

Such was their routine every day. After having tea, they visited for a short while, and Mariah shared every bit of gossip she'd heard from the event she'd accompanied Felicity to the previous evening. Then they either worked on their embroidery, or Mariah read to Julia.

Julia had never read any books by Jane Austen, and Mariah enjoyed introducing her to this wonderful author.

The more time Mariah spent with Julia, the closer she grew to the woman. She was ever so glad she'd met her, and she would do whatever she could to make sure Julia was healthy enough to survive the birth of her child.

CHAPTER FIFTEEN

Jonah leaned his back against the wall outside Julia's bedroom and listened to Julia and Mariah's conversation. Mariah's positive response to Julia's concerns caused his heart to swell in his chest. She couldn't have said anything more reassuring than the words she'd chosen. Jonah had only loved Mariah a small percent of the amount that was growing inside him now. He'd never met a woman as wonderful as her.

He hoped and prayed that Julia survived the birth of her child, but if she did not, she'd handpicked the perfect person to charge with the care and upbringing of her children. There wasn't anyone as ideal to be a substitute mother, to take her place.

He stepped forward and placed his outstretched arms against the railing that overlooked the marble tiles on the foyer floor below. He knew it was almost time for Mariah to leave, and he wanted to be there when she left Julia's room.

It was only a matter of a few more seconds before the door opened and Mariah stepped into the hallway.

"Good afternoon, Jonah," she said, then stepped around him.

"Good afternoon, Mariah. How is Julia doing?"

She stopped. "Amazingly well. I'm glad you spoke with her. She needed to know what she was facing."

"Yes. You were correct. She needed to know what might happen." He stepped closer to her. "Are you going home?"

"Yes. I promised Mama that I would accompany Felicity to the Shutter ball tonight."

"Would you mind if I walked you home?"

"That's not necessary," she said, then paused. "Unless you would like to."

"I would very much like to," Jonah answered, then placed his palm under her elbow and escorted her down the stairs and to the front door. When they reached the outdoors, he looped her arm through his and slowly accompanied her down the walk.

"I've accompanied my sister to several events, and you haven't been there," she said.

"Did you miss me?" he teased.

She laughed. "What I missed was your effort to search for a bride."

He paused, and Mariah was forced to pause beside him. She slowly lifted her gaze, and her eyes locked with the dark depths of his stare.

"I am not searching for a bride, Mariah," he said. "I have already found the person I want to make my bride."

She dropped her arm from his and took a hesitant step forward.

"You can't run away from me, sweetheart. I won't give up on you."

She spun around to face him. "You have to, Jonah. I can never marry you. It is not possible."

He reached for her, but she stepped out of his reach.

"Don't," she said as loudly as she dared, standing in the open where passersby might hear her.

BEFORE HE COULD argue with her, Mariah continued down the block. She was near her townhouse and rushed up the steps.

Jonah was close behind her. She could hear his heavy footsteps as he too rushed up the steps and strode through the door their butler held open. The second she heard the door close behind her, she felt Jonah's fingers close around hers and pull her into the nearest empty room off the foyer. He kicked the door shut behind him and pulled her into his arms.

Before she could defend herself, his mouth came down over hers and he kissed her. The kiss left no doubt as to the depth of his feelings. There was nothing left that she wanted or needed from his kiss that he did not offer her, demand from her.

His kiss deepened, then deepened even more. The passion he demonstrated commanded her to prove that she meant her refusal to marry him. But she could not. His kiss claimed every part of her heart and soul and body. It even claimed a part of her she did not know she had to give him.

He wrapped his arms around her and brought her up against him as if their bodies were one being. He skimmed his hands down her back until Mariah swore he had the power to set her flesh on fire. She was left with no will of her own, and desperation took over.

She skimmed her hands up his chest, feeling the broad expanse of his upper body and his muscled shoulders. She wrapped her arms around his neck and threaded her fingers through his thick, dark hair.

He deepened his kiss. Mariah met his advances and matched them with demands of her own. From somewhere near her, someone sighed a passionate moan. It was only a moment before she realized that someone was her.

"Mariah?" a voice called to her from beyond the door.

She pulled out of his grasp. "Mama?"

"Are you all right?"

"Yes, my lady," Jonah answered. "We are fine. We were just…discussing something."

"Is everything all right, Mariah?" her mother repeated.

"It is, Mama. Quite all right."

"Call if you need anything. Jenkins will be right outside the door."

"I will, Mama," Mariah answered, then buried her face in Jonah's chest to muffle her laughter.

She reached for Jonah's hand and pulled him toward one of the floral cushioned chairs. "Make yourself comfortable. It won't be long before Charles comes. Mama's no doubt already summoned him."

He laughed, then sat in the chair Mariah indicated. She sat on the sofa nearest him.

"We can't continue like this," she said.

"You are correct. We can't." Jonah reached for her hand and held it. "Marry me, Mariah. I cannot give you up. I will gladly give up the Darbringth title before I will give you up."

"Why are you doing this, Jonah? You know that's not possible. You may think you don't care about the title, and right now you don't. But in time, you will."

"By that time I will be so old the title will mean nothing to me or to Russell."

Before Mariah could issue another argument, the door opened and Charles entered. "Well, you two have certainly set off a hornets' nest with our mother," he said, reaching for a glass and pouring two fingers of brandy into it. Then he filled a second glass and handed it to Jonah. "Here. You look like you need this more than I do."

Jonah took the glass and drained it.

"She's still being stubborn, isn't she?" Charles said.

"Exceedingly."

"She was born stubborn, you know."

"I believe it."

"What if Julia's babe is another girl, Jonah? You know that is more than possible," Mariah said.

"Then it will be a girl," Jonah replied. "As long as it is hale and healthy, and Julia survives the birth, I don't care."

"That is today. But what about in five or ten years, when you are not as in love with me as you are now?"

"That day will never come. I will only be more in love with you."

Charles groaned. "Oh, Mariah. Please. Put this poor man out of his misery."

"Don't you side against me, Charles. You know I can't marry him. And you know why!"

Jonah sat forward in his chair. "I would like to propose a bargain, Mariah."

She considered his words with skepticism. "What sort of bargain?" she asked.

"Well, it's more an offer than a bargain."

"What sort of offer?"

"This is my proposal. If Julia has another girl, I vow I will seriously search for a wife to ensure the Darbringth line continues."

"But if Julia has a son?" she asked.

"Then you will marry me that very next day."

"But I can never give you children, Jonah."

"Do you promise to love me for the rest of my life?"

"You know I will. I already do."

"Then you will make me the happiest of men. I've loved you from the first day I met you, Mariah. Probably before then. Probably from the first day you followed Charles and me around like a lovesick puppy."

Mariah couldn't stop the tears from filling her eyes and streaming down her cheeks. "It's true, Jonah. I've loved you from the day I met you."

"Good. Then do you promise that you will marry me?"

She smiled through her tears. "Only if Julia has a son."

"I can't ask for anything more."

Jonah leaned forward and kissed Mariah in front of Charles.

Just then, the door opened and Mariah's mother stepped into the room. "Charles! Are you allowing this? I sent you down to prevent your sister from doing exactly this!"

"When has anyone ever prevented Mariah from doing anything she's made up her mind to do?" Charles said.

"That's true," their mother said, then turned and walked out of the room.

MARIAH WENT TO visit Julia every day now. The poor woman had been bedridden for two months. She could tell that Julia was more uncomfortable and that there were days when she had pain. But not once did Mariah hear her complain.

Jonah came to check on Julia every day, and often took her for short walks up and down the hall. Russell would have lived in her room full time, day in and day out, if they let him, but if Jonah didn't chase him out, Julia did. He was like a mother hen watching over her.

Mariah didn't chase him out. She could see how worried he was for his wife, and how terrified he was that he could lose her. And as the days drew nearer to when she would have her baby, Mariah was afraid of the same thing. Julia was quite large. She was uncomfortable. And she was restless.

"How are you feeling?" she asked Julia when she arrived one day early in June. They were halfway through the seventh month. Still too early to have the babe, but better than if it had come a few weeks earlier.

"My back hurts," Julia said, turning to her side. "Would you rub it?"

"I'd love to," Mariah said, leaning over the bed and rubbing Julia's back.

"I'd almost think this baby wants to be born," Julia said, "but that's not possible. It's far too early."

"How far too early?"

"At least a month," Julia answered. "It is not to be born until late in July."

"Well, I've heard that babies come when they want to. Not

when they're told they have to."

"That's true. And to be honest, I wouldn't mind if this baby decided it wanted to come early. I am ever so anxious to have this little guy out of me."

"You think it's a little guy, do you?"

"Yes, I do. It doesn't remind me of how it was with the girls." Julia smiled. "I'm sure it's a boy."

Mariah rubbed Julia's back a little longer, then stopped. "I think I'd like a cup of tea. Would you care for one, Julia?"

"I would love one."

"Then you stay right here and I'll let the kitchen know."

Mariah rushed from the room. Not because she was in a hurry to have tea sent up, but because she wanted Jonah to come check on Julia. She was afraid her friend might be going into labor.

"Are you busy?" she asked when she found him in the study. He was poring over some papers.

"What is it?"

"I think you might want to come up and check on Julia."

He got to his feet and rushed from the room. Mariah followed.

"Good afternoon, Julia," he said when he entered the room. "How are you feeling?"

"A little restless, Jonah."

He pressed on her stomach, then sat in the chair beside her bed. "How would you feel about having your baby today?" he said, relaxing in the chair.

Julia smiled. "I would love that. I've been waiting to see if this little mover and kicker is a boy or a girl."

"What do you think it is?"

"I hate to make predictions in case I'm wrong, but I don't think this baby is a girl. It just acts differently than the last five. Don't tell Russell, though, in case I'm wrong."

"I won't," Jonah promised.

Without warning, she arched on the bed when the first harsh

contraction hit her. "Yes, Jonah. I think my baby wants to make an appearance."

"Should I call for Russell to come home? He's at a meeting at the House of Lords."

"No. Let him stay as long as possible. He'll have plenty of time to pace the floors once he gets home."

"I think you're correct." Jonah reached for Julia's hand and held it. "Do you trust me, Julia?"

"Of course I trust you. Why?"

"Because I'm going to try something you've never done before."

"What?" she asked.

"It's called a cesarean section. Have you ever heard of it?"

"Y-yes. That's where you cut the mother open and remove the baby."

"Yes."

"Is it safe?"

"There are certain risks involved, but if done correctly, no more risks than a normal birth."

"Have you ever performed one before?"

Jonah shook his head. "No. I've only watched the procedure being done."

"Then I hope you watched closely and took copious notes."

"I did."

Jonah looked at Mariah and smiled. But the smile didn't reach his eyes. He was frightened. It was obvious.

"Mariah, would you call for a tea tray and a bottle of whiskey?"

"Whiskey? Do you intend to get me drunk, Jonah?" Julia asked.

"I intend for both of us to get falling-down drunk. Especially you. And me, after I deliver your baby."

"Oh, this should be interesting. I've never been drunk before."

"Then this will surely be interesting. We'll have to ask you several questions about Russell. I need some good gossip to blackmail him with."

"You wouldn't," she said. Then she giggled. "Oh, you would."

"Most definitely."

The tea came, along with the whiskey. Mariah filled a cup almost half full of tea, then Jonah added the whiskey to it.

"This is quite good," Julia said after she'd taken a sip. She took another sip. "Are you going to have some, Mariah?"

"No," Jonah said firmly. "Someone has to stay sober."

"Oh, yes," she said on a laugh, then took another sip.

"Stay with her," he told Mariah. "Keep her drinking the whiskey. I'll be right back."

He left the room for a while and came back with a bottle with clear liquid in it. In the meantime, Mariah sat with Julia while the contractions came closer together and more violently.

Julia's cries of pain escalated.

"Tell the staff to prepare for a baby," Jonah instructed a maid.

While they waited, Mariah helped Jonah cover the bed with a rubber sheet. The inebriated Julia rolled like a rag doll as they pushed and prodded the sheet into place.

Now that the task was done, Jonah rolled up his shirt sleeves, donned a long apron, and washed his hands and arms in hot, soapy water. She'd never seen a doctor take such care with cleanliness and sanitation.

He also sanitized Julia's belly where he intended to make the incision.

"Is she still out?" he asked.

"Yes."

"Good. Thankfully, she was a cheap drunk, which means she won't feel quite so horrible when she wakes."

Jonah set a vial of laudanum on the bedside table. Pointing to it, he said to Mariah, "If you see her eyelids even begin to flutter, slip this glass dropper under her tongue and squeeze twice. Just twice, understand?"

Mariah nodded, swallowed, and grew suddenly hot. She prayed she wouldn't faint, wouldn't leave Jonah without the help he needed. But laudanum! What if she turned Julia into a—

At the same moment she was becoming aware of her growing panic, she felt Jonah's hand descend on hers. "Only two drops, Mariah. You yourself have taken far more than that and never became dependent. Neither will Julia. I promise."

She swallowed her fear and turned to face him. He was so wonderfully caring, so aware of what she was feeling, and she loved him for it. His penetrating eyes searched hers, and when he smiled, he showed no doubt that she had the courage needed in order to be his steady right hand.

Straightening, she gave him a brisk nod and felt her racing heartbeat slow.

Jonah checked Julia's pulse and breathing, and, with a long intake of breath, he said, "Let's begin."

He made the incision across Julia's belly and prepared to remove the baby. Mariah held a clean towel in her hands and was prepared to take the baby when Jonah gave it to her.

She was so mesmerized by his careful, confident work that it seemed mere seconds before he said, "Here's the baby, Mariah. It's a boy."

Mariah gasped, holding this squirming new life in her hands, and her entire body responded to the miracle of it.

Jonah cut the cord, and Mariah wrapped the baby in a warm blanket, before placing the precious bundle in the arms of the staff member waiting to clean the infant, who was mewling softly now.

Jonah moved as though he intended to close the incision, then stopped. "Another towel, Mariah! Get another towel!"

At the urgency of his tone she ran for another towel and tried to place it in his hands. But he waved her away, and then she saw why. Jonah removed a second baby from Julia's belly and placed it in Mariah's arms.

It was another boy.

"Be sure to tie a ribbon around the first baby's ankle," he said to the staff.

Mariah focused on Jonah's face and saw that his eyes were filled with tears.

"Twins," he said. "An heir and a spare."

Both baby boys were crying so loudly now that Mariah was sure they could be heard all over London.

"Yes," she said as tears streamed down her own face. "An heir and a spare."

"Get me some clean water," he ordered her. "And more bandages. And my needle and satin thread. And alcohol."

The staff scattered in all directions and came back with everything Jonah needed. Meanwhile, Jonah made short work of caring for the remaining issues.

"This is the most important part," he said to Mariah. "We have to make sure everything is kept completely sanitary. That's what the British surgeon Joseph Lister said. He created an antiseptic using carbolic acid. I made some up just last week, and we need to use it now. It will help prevent surgical infections."

Jonah used the antiseptic liberally, then sewed the tidy wound. Just when he was finished, the door flew open and Russell rushed into the room.

"She's fine, Russell. She's still asleep, and your sons are over there," Jonah said, pointing to one cradle and one hastily converted dresser drawer that were squalling in the corner.

"Son?"

"No, Russell. Sons! You have your heir and your spare."

Mariah and Jonah watched as Russell crumpled to the floor in a dead faint.

CHAPTER SIXTEEN

J ONAH WATCHED OVER Julia for the next two weeks and scarcely left her side. He couldn't believe the births had gone so smoothly. Both babies were as healthy as could be, and the mother recovered remarkably fast. Of course, he refused to let her get out of bed, and Russell and the staff treated her as if she were an invalid—which she was, in certain respects.

Later on, when he was sure her incision was healing adequately, Jonah allowed her to sit in a chair and hold her babies, one at a time.

Eventually, he allowed her to stand, then walk across the room to where her sons slept. But she was not allowed to pick them up. If she wanted to hold them, a staff member would wait until she was seated again, then give her one baby at a time. Of course, she thought Jonah was being overprotective, but he gave her no choice until she was finally forced to give in to his demands or face his wrath.

When it came to naming the babies, Julia insisted that one be called Jonah. Mariah thought that was a wonderful idea, even if Jonah told his brother and his wife that wasn't necessary. They named the other boy Lance, after Julia's father.

From the day the babes were born, Mariah had tried her best to avoid being alone with Jonah. He knew her absence was intentional, and he knew why. He also knew if he didn't force her to face the promise she'd made to him, she would use every trick at her disposal to avoid keeping it.

But he was not going to allow her to do that. He refused to allow her to put off for one more day the bargain they'd struck. She had promised that she would marry him if Julia had a boy, and he intended to force her to keep her promise. The fact that Julia had presented her husband with *two* sons made the promise doubly binding.

He waited until she came to visit Julia, then caught her on the way out of the house. "There you are," he said, coming up behind her. He leaned over her shoulder and kissed her on the neck. "Were you trying to avoid me?"

"I would never try to avoid you. Never."

"Good, because I want you to go for a carriage ride with me."

"Where?"

"Through Hyde Park."

Jonah saw alarm force the color from her face.

"But Hyde Park will be the most crowded at this hour. Everyone who wants to be noticed will be there."

"Which is why that is where we need to be."

He didn't give her a chance to ignore his invitation. He took her by the arm and escorted her out the door and down the walk. His carriage was waiting in front of the house, and he helped her inside. Of course, his carriage did not have the top up, so they were easily seen by everyone.

The second they were settled, the driver jingled the reins and they were off to Hyde Park.

"I wanted to talk to you, Jonah."

"About what, Mariah?"

"This."

"What? About riding through Hyde Park?"

"No. About going through with the promises we made to each other."

"Do you mean the promise that you made me, stating that you would marry me if Julia had a son?"

She lowered her gaze to her lap. "Yes, that promise."

"Look up, sweetheart. We're entering the park. We are about to be seen by all of London."

"Oh, Jonah," she sighed. "Turn around. Let's go home."

He smiled, then lifted her hand to his lips and kissed her fingers. "That's not possible, Mariah. Now, you were saying?" he said, forcing her to bring her doubts and fears into the open.

"I want you to know that I don't intend to force you to honor the commitment we made to each other."

"You don't?"

"Of course I don't. I know that you were only teasing me."

"Is that what you think my kisses meant? That I was teasing you?"

"No," she said, lowering her gaze again. "I think that you truly meant them, at the time."

"At the time?"

"Yes."

"Are you insinuating that I am able to turn my feelings on and off in the blink of an eye?"

"Well. No. Maybe. Oh," she sighed in frustration. "I don't know."

"Well, I know. I am not one who changes with the wind. Those are my feelings. And to prove it..." Jonah reached inside his jacket pocket and brought out a small box. He opened it and held it in front of her.

She looked at the box in his hand. "Oh, Jonah. This is beautiful."

"It's a pearl surrounded by diamonds—because you are a pearl, and in my eyes, you are more precious than diamonds."

"Oh! Oh my! It's beautiful." Mariah lowered her gaze again. "But I can't marry you."

"Why can't you marry me, Mariah?"

"Because of...because I can't..."

"Can't give me what I want? Is that it? Mariah! How do you know you have nothing to give me? Have you asked me what I want?"

"I can't give you children, Jonah. I can't give you the one thing that every man wants."

Jonah swept off his hat, banged it on his knee, and resettled it roughly on his head. "Let me just tell you what I want, my darling. I want someone who can love me unconditionally. I want someone who will stand by me and not let me walk through life alone. And I want someone who will take care of my heart and love it for eternity. Can you do that?"

"But I can't give you children."

"If God wants us to have children, he will find a way for us to have them, Mariah. I don't need children to survive, but I do need you."

Jonah took off her glove and slid the ring on her finger. "Please. Love me. I don't know how I'll live if you don't love me."

She slowly locked her tear-filled gaze with his. "I do," she answered. "I do love you."

Jonah gasped. These were the sweetest four words he had ever heard.

He held the hand that wore his ring. "I wanted to give you something special so the world would know that you are mine and that I love you."

She stared into his eyes, tears streaming down her cheeks while delicious ribbons of joy danced in her heart. "I never thought I would marry. I never believed anyone would want to marry me."

"Believe it now, my love. I cannot wait to marry you."

"When?" Mariah asked through her tears.

"Whenever you want." He reached into his pocket and pulled out another surprise. "Open it," he told her.

Mariah opened the special license.

"We can marry any time you want, and any place you want."

"Oh," she cried. "I love you, Jonah Reynolds. I love you more than the sun and the moon and the stars."

"That is almost as much as I love you," he replied, giving her a quick kiss on the cheek. "Now, where do you want to get married? And when?"

Mariah grinned. "I want to get married here. In London. So your family and mine can attend."

"That sounds perfect," he said before kissing her again. "And when would you like to get married?"

"Tomorrow. Yes, tomorrow!"

"That is perfect. I can't think of anything I'd like to do more than marry you tomorrow." Jonah kissed her on the lips right there in an open carriage in Hyde Park.

"Then we will have a party at Hope's House when we get there," she said. "We'll celebrate properly where we are going to spend the rest of our lives."

"That is the perfect place for us to start our lives," he said, placing his arm around the back of the cushion, then letting his arm slide down around her shoulders.

Mariah turned and gave him a look he hadn't seen before, and quickly removed his arm. She loved him, yes. Would she tolerate a display of that love in public? No.

"Look," she said, pointing toward the carriage approaching them. "It's my sister and Lord Pembleton."

The Pembleton carriage stopped next to theirs. "Oh, Mariah," Felicity said with a beaming smile. "I want you to be the first to know." She held up her hand and displayed a diamond. "Lord Pembleton has asked me to marry him, and I have accepted."

"Oh, congratulations, Felicity. I am so happy for you." Mariah turned and smiled at Jonah. "I also have news."

She lifted her hand and displayed the pearl and diamond ring Jonah had given her. "Dr. Reynolds has asked me to marry him tomorrow, and I have accepted."

Felicity squealed with delight. "Did you say tomorrow?"

"I did," Mariah said with an enormous smile. "We would have married today, but there's not enough time to squeeze one more massively important event into the day."

"Does Mama know?" Felicity asked.

"Not yet."

"Oh, I wager she will be so shocked she will swoon," Felicity said. "You must wait to tell her until we are there to witness it."

"Then you had best hurry. We're going there as soon as we finish our drive."

"We'll be right behind you," Felicity said as their carriage continued on its way.

"Now, let's go tell your mother our news," Jonah said.

Mariah lifted her head and kissed him on the lips. It was a discreet, brief, perfectly lovely kiss. There were too many people there that could see them to let passion rule. She had clearly demonstrated that she wasn't that brave. Yet.

➤➤➤✦◄◄◄

MARIAH WOKE WITH a start the next morning and jumped out of bed. Today was her wedding day.

It was barely light outside, but it wouldn't be long until the wedding would take place. Perhaps she should have given herself one more day to prepare.

Then she smiled. No, she'd waited nearly thirty years to get married. She didn't want to wait one day longer.

She'd stayed up half the night packing her clothes and everything she wanted to take with her when they left for Hope's House. She only kept back her traveling clothes and a few last-minute and special items that she didn't trust to travel in a wagon.

Jonah was in charge of arranging for a clergyman to perform the ceremony, and the kitchen staff had been up all night preparing the food that would be served at the wedding breakfast.

Felicity had promised to get several flower arrangements for the house, and a bouquet for the bride. But Charles had the most important task. He was charged with getting Jonah's wedding band.

Jonah had told her he didn't need a ring, but Mariah wouldn't hear of it. She wanted the world to know that Jonah belonged to her, and that she belonged to him.

Time flew with unbelievable speed, and before she knew it, it was time to go to her room and dress. She didn't have a wedding gown per se, but she had a gown she'd known she would wear if she ever managed to marry, and she put it on with the greatest care.

She was nearly ready to go down to the formal drawing room when there was a knock on the door. "Enter," she said, expecting her mother, or perhaps her sister.

But it wasn't either of them. When the door opened, Charles stood in the open doorway.

"I was going to ask if you were happy, Mari, but I can see from the radiant glow on your face that you are extremely happy."

"I am, Charles. I've never been happier."

"Then I am ever so happy for you. You couldn't have found a more perfect man, Mari. Be happy. Always."

Mariah stepped into Charles's arms and gave her big brother a sincere hug, then looked at him through a river of tears of love.

"Are you ready to get married?"

"Yes, Charlie. I've been ready my whole life."

"Then allow me the honor of escorting you."

He held out his arm, and Mariah placed her hand on his sleeve. And he took her down to be married.

MARIAH'S WEDDING WAS perfect. It was small, and intimate, and...perfect.

Her family was all there, as well as Jonah's family. Julia stood up with her, and Russell stood up with Jonah.

After the ceremony, they all enjoyed a delicious breakfast

before Jonah and Mariah bade their families and guests goodbye.

They knew it would be late before they arrived at Hope's House, but that was the least of their worries. They were too happy to be concerned over the time.

"Do you know how happy I am?" she said as they made their way through the countryside.

"Yes, I do. Because I am just as happy. I knew the minute I saw you after all those years of being away that you were the perfect woman for me."

"What if Julia had two more girls instead of two boys?"

"It wouldn't have mattered, Mariah. I would have married you anyway."

"But I couldn't have married you."

"Then I would have had to kidnap you and forced you to marry me."

She laughed. "No, you wouldn't have."

"Yes, I would have, Mariah. It's a rare happening when you meet the woman of your dreams. I knew from the minute I saw you again that you were the other half of my heart and soul. That happens so seldom in life that when it does, you have to make sure you don't lose the person that makes you whole."

"Oh, Jonah. I felt the same about you, but you realize you are on the short side of this bargain. No matter what you think I can give you, I can't give you children. I will always regret that."

"I won't. As long as I have your love, I don't need anything else."

She placed her head on his shoulder. "You will always have my love, Jonah. Always and forever."

Jonah lowered his head and kissed her, and that kiss was the most heartfelt one she'd ever received.

They reached Hope's House shortly before nightfall and greeted the staff to let them know that they were home. A hasty telegram the night before the wedding had alerted Hope's House to the change in marital status. All seemed perfectly thrilled.

They feasted on leftover food that the cook had fixed for

dinner, then went to their suite of rooms—the same rooms where Mariah had stayed when she was here with Charles.

This was Jonah and Mariah's wedding night. She had waited a lifetime for this night—a night she never thought she would have.

They gave their bodies to each other the same as they would night after night for the rest of their earthly union and rejoiced in the turn that their lives had taken.

CHAPTER SEVENTEEN

D AY BY DAY, Jonah and Mariah settled into a comfortable routine of married life. He took in a steady stream of patients that needed to be cured. She helped him with anything she could. She visited with the patients who were going through recovery and tried to give them all the positive support she could.

She helped with the updating of Hope's House, and added to the library and the room where the people went to wile away their time. Keeping them from becoming bored was one of the most important parts of the recovery process.

At night they took time to eat dinner together, then sat together in their sitting room and talked over the day's events, or took a walk in the garden. They made leisurely love before falling asleep. Life was idyllic.

Mariah was helping in the dining room after the noon meal, which she did often, when Jonah came to her.

"How would you like to take a drive over to Jack and Annie's?"

"I'd love to," she said. "I wrote to them and told them we married, but we haven't been to see them since."

"I know," he said. "I received a note from Jack this morning stating that he's been looking for my obituary in the paper, since he hasn't heard from us in so long he thought one or both of us had to be dead."

Mariah laughed at Jack's humor.

"Get your wrap and let's take a drive."

A servant brought her wrap and bonnet, and they bounced off in the carriage. When they arrived, Jack and Annie were waiting for them with their cloaks on.

"What's this?" Mariah asked when they approached the carriage.

"Well," Jack said, "we decided that since you hadn't been to see us, you probably hadn't been to see Jack and Livie yet, either. So we decided to grab you before you got out of your carriage, and all go to see them."

"Oh," Mariah said. "That's a wonderful idea. Jonah's been so busy, we haven't had time to do much at all except take care of patients."

"Yes," Jack teased. "I remember how busy Annie and I were immediately after our wedding."

She felt her cheeks turn warm when everyone laughed.

Annie and Jack stepped into the carriage, and he closed the door behind them. Mariah was glad Jonah had chosen their largest carriage.

The trip to Angel's Wings Orphanage took a little longer than it had taken to reach Jack and Annie's, but the four of them talked the entire way, and it didn't seem to take long at all. Before Mariah knew it, they had turned into the lane and pulled up in front of the orphanage.

Jack and Livie came out to greet them and invited them in for a cup of tea. Jonah had written them to tell them that he and Mariah were married, and they were as happy for the new couple as they could be.

They all spent the afternoon at the orphanage, then took a tour of the gardens. The berries and fruits were ripe now, and the women from the church and from town were in the workroom preparing jams and jellies.

They watched them for a while, then Jonah chose several varieties to take with them to Hope's House. He promised to send them the money for the treats when they returned home, and surprised his friend with a standing order for the hospital.

When they finished in the fruit room, Livie asked, "Would you like to go upstairs and visit the babies?"

"Yes," Mariah said, knowing that it would be hard to see the babies, yet knowing that she couldn't pass up the opportunity.

"Come with me," Livie said, and led the way to the nursery.

Mariah was surprised that Jack and Jonah followed them. She'd expected them to return to the receiving room while she and Livie went up another flight of stairs.

"Has anyone adopted little Allison?" she asked.

"No, not yet. But I expect her to get adopted soon. She's too adorable to be overlooked much longer."

When they reached the nursery, Mariah went directly to Allison's cradle and looked down on her.

"Is this one Allison?" Jonah asked.

"Yes," she answered, then held out her hand. The baby grabbed her finger and held on to it. "She's beautiful. Even prettier than the last time I was here."

"Here," Jonah said. "Let me see her."

Mariah watched as Jonah picked her up and held her. He placed her in one arm, then shifted her to the other arm.

"What are you doing, Jonah?" she asked.

"I'm just making sure she fits."

"Fits what?"

"Fits in my arms."

Mariah looked at her husband as if he'd lost his mind.

He didn't say anything, just looked at Livie and smiled. "Yes, Livie. We'll take this one," he said, handing the child back to Mariah. "Do you have any more? Preferably boys, a little older?"

"Jonah?" Mariah said. What was he doing?

"I do, Jonah," Livie said. "I just happen to have two little boys, one two and one four, who look a great deal like this little girl. I think they are probably brothers and sister."

"Could we see them, too?"

"Of course. I'll go get them."

Livie left the room, and Mariah looked at Jonah with a confused expression. "Jonah, what are you doing?"

"I'm picking out our family, Mariah. You said you wanted children, and I can't think of a better way to get them."

She looked at Jack and realized he was standing back covering his mouth to hide his laughs. She turned back to Jonah. "Are you serious?"

"Of course I'm serious. This is no joking matter. You just tell me if I've picked one out that you don't like, and I'll put it back."

Mariah nestled little Allison closer to her and held on tightly. "Jonah! For heaven's sake. We don't window-shop for babies! We'll keep this one."

Just then, Livie walked into the room with a little boy in each hand. "This is Tommy," she said, holding up the littlest boy's hand. "He's two years old."

"Hi, Tommy," Jonah said. Instead of answering, Tommy hid behind Livie's skirt. "And what's your name?" Jonah asked the older boy, hunching down.

"My name is Marcus. Are you going to take my sister home with you?" the child asked.

"I don't know, Marcus. Do you think I should take her home?"

"Will you be nice to her?"

Jonah smiled. "Oh, yes, Marcus. We'll be very nice to her. My wife is a really nice lady."

"Are you a nice man?"

"Yes. I'm nice too."

"Then yes, you can take her with you."

"Do you look after your brother and your sister?"

"Yes. My mum said that's what I had to do."

"Your mum was right. Big brothers should always look after their brothers and sisters."

"That's what she said," Marcus replied. "Did you bring us in here so we could say bye to our sister?"

"No," Jonah said. "Actually, we brought you in so you could ask your sister if you could go with her."

"But she can't talk. She's too little."

"Then you'll have to answer for her."

"Really?"

"Yes. What do you think she'd say if I asked her if you and Tommy could come with her?"

"Oh," Marcus said excitedly. "She'd say yes! She's never gone anywhere without us."

"Then I guess we'll have to take you and Tommy home with us."

"Did you hear that, Tommy? We get to go with Allie. The man said we could."

The little boy stepped around Livie's skirt to run to his brother and hug him tightly.

"Now," Jonah said, "I want you to meet the nice lady who is going to take care of you. Her name is Mariah, but you can call her Mari if you'd like."

Mariah knelt down so she was eye level with the two little boys and held their hands in hers.

"Hello, Marcus. Hello, Tommy. Would you like to come home with us?"

"We'd like that very much, but why are you cryin'? Don't you want us to come home with you?" Marcus said.

"I want you to come home with me very much. I'm crying because I'm so very happy."

"Oh," Marcus said with a confused expression on his face.

Jonah put his hands on his boys' shoulders and led them from the room. Mariah followed with baby Allie in her arms.

They went down the stairs and out the door of the orphanage. Jack and Annie were already in the carriage waiting, and Jonah lifted the children up and placed them on the seat beside Jack. Then he turned to assist Mariah inside. When she was settled next to Annie, he handed her the baby. A small basket of clothing and baby paraphernalia was next, tucked behind the seat.

"Thank you, Livie," Mariah said. "I don't know what to say. This has been one of the happiest days of my life."

"Hopefully, the happiest day was the day you married me," Jonah said on a laugh.

"It was. It definitely was," she said.

They bade Jack and Annie goodbye, and the carriage rambled forward.

＞＞＞＜＜＜

IT WAS LATE when they arrived back at Hope's House. Marcus, Tommy, and the baby had all fallen asleep. When Jonah and Mariah carried them into the house, several of the staff ran forward to help get the children settled for the night.

"I should have given you fair warning of what Livie and I had decided to do, but I wanted it to be a surprise," Jonah said.

"It was definitely a surprise," Mariah said before tucking the two boys into one bed and removing the clothes from one of the drawers to make a cradle for little Allie.

"If I had told you, then our baby wouldn't have to sleep in a drawer, and would have a proper cradle to sleep in. What was I thinking?"

Mariah tucked a blanket around Allie and stepped back to see their children asleep in their beds. Tears glistened in her eyes.

"I never thought I'd have a family, Jonah," she said when he stepped close to her and wrapped his arm around her shoulders.

"I know you didn't," he said, "which is why I kept what I was going to do a secret. If anything had gone wrong, it would have been just too painful for you."

"I'm glad you did, though," she said. "It made the surprise an unbelievable event."

They looked down on their little family, finding it impossible to step away just yet. "How many children did you always think you wanted?" Jonah asked her after he kissed her on the forehead.

"I'd never really thought about it. I only knew I wanted a large family."

"Large, as in how many?"

"Six, maybe. Or seven, or eight."

Jonah laughed loudly. "Eight, you say?"

"Or maybe nine."

"Oh, heaven help us, Mari. If you are going for nine, we might as well aim for an even dozen."

"Oh, that sounds perfect," she said on a laugh. "You have to admit, this is the easiest way to have a family. You just go to the orphanage and pick one out."

Jonah laughed again, then pulled her into his arms and held her against him. "I love you, Mariah. I can't even tell you how much I love you. Nor can I tell you how perfectly things have turned out."

"I feel the same, Jonah. I've loved you since you first came to see Charles."

"That's when I fell in love with you, except I wasn't smart enough to realize it yet. I had to wait until I thought I might never get you to realize how desperately I needed you."

"Well, we know now," she said.

"And we'll remind each other every day so we never forget."

"No, we'll never forget."

CHAPTER EIGHTEEN

A YEAR AFTER they brought Marcus, Tommy, and Alli home, they increased their family by one—a little girl named Josie.

The year after that, a young lass had twin boys, Frank and Richard, who they called Ricky.

Livie had tried to find homes for the twins, but no one wanted two babes at the same time, at least no one with several children already. Because Jonah and Mariah already had four children, she didn't reach out to them until she'd exhausted all other possibilities.

The twins were already three months old, so the decision to take them wasn't difficult at all. They weren't newborns, but older babes.

Jonah wasn't sure what difference that made, but Mariah guaranteed him he wouldn't even realize there were two more additions to their family. There were always patients or patients' parents who jumped at the chance to hold one of the babes, or feed them, or play with them. And Mariah was always ready to accommodate these patients and hand one of the younger ones over.

Nearly a year after they'd taken in Frank and Ricky, a missive came in the post from Livie. It was addressed to Mariah.

Jonah held the letter in his hands for several moments, then put it in his jacket pocket. He had a feeling he knew why Livie had written Mariah. She had another baby or two that needed homes. But he wasn't sure they were ready to take in more babies. He needed to consider this carefully.

What he meant was that he wasn't sure if Mariah was ready to take on any more babies. He was consumed with his patients all day, and the main responsibility for the care and nurturing of the children fell on her shoulders.

The letter from Livie burned a hole in his pocket all during dinner with his family. He looked around their table and saw the six children at their seats. They were growing so fast. Soon they'd be old enough to care for themselves, and Mariah could finally have a minute to herself.

He placed his hand over the letter and decided not to show it to her. Yes, that would be the sensible thing to do. That would be the kindest thing for Mariah.

Dinner was over, and Mariah took the children up to their rooms. This was her favorite time of the day. Jonah always tried to join her. She gathered them around her and read them a story, then they said their prayers. After their nighttime prayers, they went to their own rooms, and she and Jonah told them goodnight. They kissed each one and told them how much they loved them, how glad Mariah and Jonah were that they were their children.

Then they blew out the candles and went downstairs.

The next hour or so was Jonah's time alone with Mariah. Sometimes she stayed awake so they could talk, and sometimes she fell asleep with her head on his shoulder. He'd always loved her, but when they had time alone together, he realized he loved her more than ever.

Tonight, however, Mariah took his hand and led him out to the garden.

"Oh, we haven't sat out here for a long time," he said.

"I know. I've missed sitting on our bench in the moonlight."

"Me too," he said. "It's so peaceful here."

"Yes," she sighed, then turned to look at him. "So, when are you going to show me what you have in your pocket?"

"How do you know I have something in my pocket?"

"Oh, Jonah. I'm not sure there's anything you can hide from me."

He sat on the bench and pulled her back into his arms. "Are you sure you want to see it?"

"Of course I want to see it," she said. "It's from Livie, isn't it?"

"Yes, but before you read it, don't you think we should discuss things?"

"What things?"

"Having more children," he said.

"Don't you want more children?"

"What I want isn't the point," he said. "I'd take the entire orphanage if we could. But I'm not the one who has to make sure they have clothes to wear, and food to eat, and has to put them to bed each night. I get to come to their rooms and listen to you read them a story, then say their prayers with them, and kiss them good night. You shoulder the brunt of the work, Mari."

"And I love it. Don't you know that?"

Jonah breathed a heavy sigh, then reached into his pocket and removed the letter. He handed it to his wife, then waited while she read it beneath the lantern by the bench.

He watched as she read the letter again. Her eyes filled with tears, then spilled over her lashes. She wiped her eyes and handed him the letter. He slowly read it, and before he reached the bottom, he knew their family would be growing. And not by one or two or three, but by four.

"So, when do you want to go for them?"

"You don't mind, do you?" she asked through her tears.

"Of course not. We *have* to take them."

"The poor dears. To lose their mother and father and two siblings in a carriage accident and have no family left. They think they are all alone in the world."

"This won't be easy, Mari. Two of them are still babes, so they won't remember so much. But the older two will feel the loss of their parents and siblings and need us to help them get over it."

"And we will. All eight of us."

Jonah laughed. "That's a staggering number, Mariah. All *eight* of us. And with four more, it will be twelve. All *twelve* of us!"

"For someone who was convinced she'd never have children, you've made me the happiest person alive. I love you, Jonah."

"Not as much as I love you, Mari. Not nearly as much."

And he kissed her to prove how much he loved her.

About the Author

Laura Landon taught high school for ten years before leaving the classroom to open her own ice-cream shop. As much as she loved serving up sundaes and malts from behind the counter, she closed up shop after penning her first novel. Now she spends nearly every waking minute writing, guiding her heroes and heroines to find their happily ever afters.

She is the author of more than a dozen historical novels, including SILENT REVENGE, INTIMATE DECEPTION, and her newest Montlake Romance release, INTIMATE SURRENDER.

Her books are enjoyed by readers around the world.

CPSIA information can be obtained
at www.ICGtesting.com
Printed in the USA
BVHW050936030123
655400BV00010B/209